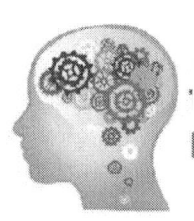

Educate.Write.Collaborate

Editors
Kemi Elufiede
Jacquie Skokna

Illustrator
Elaine Wood

Cover Design
Carissa Barker-Stucky

3

Preface

Dear Reader,

Carnegie Writers, Inc. (CW) is pleased to present its 6th publication, *Strangers: A collection* in collaboration with Nashville Community Education. With your support, CW can continue to extend community-based programming by offering the Adult Author Workshop.

This creative anthology includes a diverse and unique literature selections of various genres, such as poetry, short stories, article writing, playwriting, and collaborative writing. Because of your support, CW can continue to motivate writers through self-expression.

Thank you,

Kemi Elufiede

Table of Authors

Holly Achurch..228
Mildred Bledsoe...................................6 & 255
Stephanie Grattan............................17 & 255
Dennis Greeno...................................35 & 255
Chelsea Champion....................................44
James Currey......................................54 & 203
Tom Jamison..228
Kelly Key...66
Julie Kramer..81 & 203
Brenda North...99
Denise Sheehan.........................125 & 228
Steven Sheehan....................................132
Louan Tillman....................................137 & 203
Mike Wargo...154
Elaine Wood..171
Scott Wiley...178
Progressive Stories...............................202

Mildred O. Bledsoe retired in December 2010 from the State of Tennessee, Department of Education. She received her Bachelor's degree in Liberal Studies from Middle Tennessee State University. She has served on the board of directors for a nonprofit organization, Solid Faith Outreach Ministries since 2013. Currently, she is working on her new book, *How She Survived Domestic Violence*. Mildred currently lives in LaVergne, Tennessee and she enjoys encouraging others, cooking, travelling, and meeting new friends.

A Poem of Comfort

"Beyond This"
Suffering, heartaches, and pains,
I have gone, beyond this.
When restless nights seem only to exist,
I have gone, beyond this.

Joy and Happiness, one day will be mine.
God shall whisper to me, peace be thine
Be it resolved, as I take my rest,
I have gone through some trials, and past
my test.

Cry if you must, as the pain is real.
Do not let others tell you how you should
feel.

Please know that your tears are not a sign
that you are weak. On the contrary, my
love, they give you temporary relief.

Relief through sorrow, pain, and grief
Remember to look up with faith and belief.
You all loved me, but God loved me best
I have gone "Beyond This," to take my rest.

The Invasion of the Innocent

The innocent was helpless.
Against the strength in the dark,
where the invaders lurked.
With a deliberate heart.

The invaders speech was quiet with no
remark. Their grips were like the bite of a
shark.

From childhood, the innocent felt shame
and despair. Low self-esteem was the
outcome, from jokes about a girl with no
hair.

There was no experience of a teenage life.
Innocent went from playing dolls, mud pies,
and dress up. To being pregnant and a
young housewife.

What kind of world is this where the innocent live? A place where people are not eager to forgive.

A location of sorrow filled with pain and grief, where tears of the weary need more than a handkerchief.

In a world that spins round and round, where the innocent is filled with ups and downs. Emotions are bruised and wounds run deep. It is the recklessness of others; the innocent fails to get much sleep.

Where can the innocent run?
On the other hand, to whom can they turn?
I heard that there is a place of refuge in the garden, where life first begun.

The innocent is exposed to strangers both near and far. Like the spreading of gravel, once it is covered with tar. They become acquainted though harsh, as it seems. The innocent and the invader have now become one as a picture in a frame.

The Cake Rose:
Just Before the Night Fell

Mary Davis was born May 18, 1913. Her parents
were Jock and Johnny Davis. She had a twin, whose
name was Anna. Mary was one of six children. She
grew up in Franklin, Tennessee. The only facts we
have regarding her childhood is that she did not
graduate from high school, and was married at the
age of eighteen.

Mrs. Davis-Blackman was a short and stocky woman.
Her salt and pepper hair was shoulder length and felt
like silk to touch. She wore black and gold rim
eyeglasses. She had a happy home. She is
remembered today for her faith in God, love for
family, and her cake baking.

Mrs. Davis-Blackman was a wonderful housewife and
mother. Mary was friendly, caring, and devoted to
her family and to the cause of Christ. During her
short life's journey, she bore fifteen children. She
had two sets of twins Jerry and Geraldine; and
Annette and Jennett. The rest of her children were
single births. Their names are John T. Jr.; Mary E.;
Tommy T.; James E.; Carl; Roy; Isiah; Mildred K.;
Rosetta; and Carolyn A. Blackman. Mary was a quiet
spoken woman. Nevertheless, she was one who
spoke with authority and power. She said what she
meant, and meant what she said. Mrs. Blackman did

10

not spare the rod when it came to disciplining her children. She loved her family at all times, even when it came to discipline. She often said, "It is going to hurt me just as much as it hurts you."

Her husband called her blessed, and cherished the time that they shared together. She prayed about everything, and trusted in God through the process. Mary stayed at home and cared for the children, while her husband, John worked for the L & N Railroad, (Radnor Yard). She was known for baking cakes from scratch. Her daily routine was consistent.

She rose from bed at 5:00 a.m., made her way to the kitchen, put on a pot of water for coffee, and proceeded to prepare breakfast. Breakfast usually consisted of sausage, eggs, fried potatoes, and homemade biscuits. Her husband ate breakfast first and then the children would enter the kitchen to eat. She really knew how to cook. She often made Blackberry cobbler, fried chicken with gravy, fried corn, and buttermilk bread.

During the week, Mary wore house-dresses and old shoes that she walked on the back-heel part of the shoes. She kept her salt and pepper hair pulled back behind her ears. Also, she talked to her mother every day as they watched the "Soaps on TV." Saturday was her wash day. It was not strange to see Mary and the children going to do laundry. The laundry mat was about three city blocks from their

11

house. The children would carry pillowcases filled with dirty clothes, while some of them shared the responsibility of toting a number 10 tub filled with dirty clothes and linen. One thing I can say about Mary is she did not ask anyone to do anything that she would not do herself.

Mary and her husband went to church every Sunday, along with their children. She was an Usher and sang in the choir. She often sang hymns and prayed during worship service. This was a woman of great faith. During times when finances were gone, and the meal barrel was low, we would hear her praying for God to bless us with food, and before the day was over, someone would bring food and clothing for our family. After many years, her husband became a preacher, and was an Associate Pastor of a prominent church in Nashville, Tennessee.

On Sunday, July 2, 1967, Mary had an unusual day. Breakfast was different; she served fried chicken, gravy, fried apples, and homemade biscuits. She cleaned up the kitchen and got dressed for church. On that Sunday, she went to Franklin since it was their homecoming. Mrs. Davis-Blackman was extremely happy to be at her home town church. She and the family stayed until late in the evening. Once church was over, she and her family traveled back to Nashville. They talked and laughed all the way home.

In those days, people did not cook or do domestic work on Sunday. They would prepare Sunday dinner on Saturday night and reheat the meal on Sunday after church. Therefore, it was not her normal routine to bake a cake on Sunday night. Once the family was in the house and settled, Mary proceeded to the kitchen where she positioned the oven racks in the center of the oven. Then she turned on the oven to 400 degrees F in order to preheat the oven as she gathered the ingredients to make a yellow cake with chocolate icing.

I could see her as she went to the cabinet, and proceeded to get the ingredients needed for the cake. At first, she got the baking powder, sugar, flour, salt and vanilla flavoring off the shelf, and placed them on the table. Secondly, she went to the refrigerator and got the eggs and milk, and placed them on the table. Now she is looking in the cupboard located underneath the sink and got the sifter, rolling pin and two cake pans. Finally, she got the large green glass bowl, a measuring cup, measuring spoons, along with a large wooden spoon that she used for stirring and mixing.

She is in the kitchen with flour on her hands, after sifting the flour, baking powder, and salt into a large green mixing bowl. The eggs are on the table so that they will reach room temperature. She poured the milk into the measuring cup, and the vanilla flavoring is still in its original bottle. Once the eggs reached room temperature Mary poured the milk into the dry mixture and began to break the eggs open and mix them into the batter one at a time. The vanilla flavoring is the last ingredient that she added to the mixture prior to placing the cakes in the oven.

Mary lightly coated two 8-inch cake pans with butter and dusted them with all-purpose flour to prevent the cake from sticking to the bottom and sides of the pan. Mary is now ready to pour the batter into the pans as she sang a familiar song. She opened the oven door slowly and placed the two cake pans on the middle shelf. She was very careful in order not to allow the oven door to slam shut because the slightest jarring of the oven would cause the cake to fall. Therefore, she held the oven door and gently closed the door. It was not long before the aroma of the baking cake filled the house. Everyone was anxiously waiting for the cake to rise. After 45 minutes, the cake was ready. Mother took the cake out of the oven to let it cool down.

I find it fascinating how Mary's life resembles the cake that she was making. For 54 years, Mary has been gathering ingredients for life. She had an unmeasurable amount of kindness; compassion; love, and faith that fueled her every day. One of her favorite songs was, "Keep on pushing," by the Impressions, released in 1964. She had a portion of mercy on those who were less fortunate, and bestowed grace on those who were in trouble. Mary's cup was overflowing with thanksgiving and forgiveness. She knew that prayer was her main ingredient and once stirred with faith, she was ready to go through the fires of life.

To sweeten her life, she had a bag of love that she gave out, and received it daily. Mary's spice was patience, kindness, and longsuffering along with and a pinch of peace, just to name a few.

Mary lived an enjoyable life. She was a happy homemaker; she enjoyed cooking and taking care of her children. Though sifted through out her life, Mrs. Blackman faced life challenges knowing that, "The Lord will make a way somehow." She survived thirteen pregnancies, the death of two sons, the stress of having two sons incarcerated, the burden of caring for grandchildren, along with providing guidance to her four minor children.

Sunday, July 2, 1967 was a peculiar day. Mary was doing things that she had never done before. She baked a cake, rode with my daddy to take my brother to work at 10:30 P.M. She arrived home at about 11:35 p.m. Mary did not get a chance to finish the cake before she went to bed. It was her intention to put the icing on the next morning. However, there was no way for her to know that she would not see another day.

Sadly, Mary rose early the next morning and collapsed on the bathroom floor. James picked her up and laid her on the bed. She tried to speak, but no one could understand what she was trying to say. Consequently, my daddy took mother to the emergency room at Vanderbilt Hospital. Upon arriving at the hospital, the doctor admitted her to the critical unit. She was in critical condition for about five hours.

It was about 11:00 a.m. when my daddy and sisters returned from the hospital and gave us the sad news, "Mother is gone."

"The Cake rose before the night fell," Mary has fallen into her eternal night. The cake was sitting on a wire rack. Waiting for mother to come back. The icing was missing for all to see my Mother's smile is all the icing I need.

Stephanie Grattan is a Pre-K teacher and Children's Program Coordinator for the Brentwood Library. She has been writing poetry and short stories for the last 15 years. She currently resides in South Nashville with her boyfriend, Kevin.

Read All About It:

Nashville Libraries Quest for Early Literacy

In an age where funding for public programs is being cut left and right, what program can report a 97% success rating and national recognition? Ask any five-year old in Nashville. Bringing Books to Life, a program stated by the Nashville Public Library has spent the last fourteen years creating a love of books in some of the city's youngest readers.

Started in 2003, Bringing Books to Life (BBTL) is a community resource serving Pre-K children in Nashville and Davidson county. BBTL partners with teachers, parents, and any preschool or daycare center within Davidson county, teaching and mentoring them in creating literacy-based activities that inspire children's innate love of play.

18

"To stoke their interest in stories, we use five simple practices from the American Library Association's Every Child Ready to Read curriculum: reading, writing, singing, talking and playing." says Liz Atack, BBTL's program coordinator. To implement this curriculum, activities include finger plays, singing, emergent reading practices like studying letter sounds, and talking to increase young ones' vocabularies.

BBTL sends a team out, based on a parent or school's request, starting with story time with an age-appropriate book. Children will then do other activities related to the story such as crafts and peer to peer book discussions. Then, the NPL's Puppet Truck will pay a visit and professional artists from Nashville's Wishing Chair Productions perform the same story the group has been studying. Atack also meets with the parents and teachers individually, "[sharing] materials and interactive activity ideas, so they can increase ALA's five literacy-based practices in their classrooms and homes."

According to the National Survey of Children's Health, it takes 1,000 hours of "lap time" for young children to have the readiness skills to learn to read. Unfortunately, it is reported that only 53% of parents in Tennessee read to their young children every day. To combat these statistics, BBTL works with families, schools, and especially at-risk communities to instill the importance of reading in not only children, but their parents as well.

NPL states that now they have served 191 schools and families and have reached an audience of more than 62,000 children and adults. They have also received the Marshall Cavendish Excelle in Library Programming Award and Liz Atack was named the 2014 Toyota Teacher of the Year by the National Center for Families Learning, the first librarian to win in the award's 17-year history.

The results speak for themselves. Following BBTL programs, 99% of parent participants report knowing more about their child's literacy development and 97% report they engage in reading activities more often with their children. The Nashville Public Library has tapped into the importance and radical growth that occurs in those first five years of life and has found a fun, useful, and did we mention free (!!) resource to ensure brighter futures for our youngest residents.

Frank

Grey streets, grey sky, grey wetness all around; it was a typical New England winter day when I was born. The rain would come down in sheets during the late afternoon. As the sun went down, the rain turned to ice and everything froze over. Winter marched on and the snow would start . That first snow was always beautiful, the same magical image you saw on Christmas cards. Soft and fluffy white flakes coated everything, lights sparkling off the blank canvas gave the streets a warm glow.

For those first few hours before the snow blowers and kids in their pajamas, forced from their cozy couch snow day cocoons, would emerge, the world was perfect. When you're not from the upper eastern corner snow is novel. That perfection lasts forever, a mystical globe effect that cheers holiday spirit. When you are from the Northeast you see snow and you wait for the sludge to form. It usually only takes twenty four hours, which is why the rest of the country can delight in the fluffy stuff. The dirt mixes with the ice, mixes with the soot and ash, mixes with the stomping of boots, and that pure white magic morphs into grey, wet, slushy, sludge. Just thinking of it I can feel the wetness between my toes. I can feel the howling wind whipping through my body, the kind of cold that settles into your bones and stays around for a few months. I was born on the morning of the first snow and by late afternoon had all the magic sucked out of me. My mother lived on the streets.

She came from nothing and continued to have nothing. She grew up to have six kids and then didn't have any time either. I was the youngest, the runt of the litter. My father split before she even gave birth to me. He had taken up with one of the neighbors, he didn't even have the decency to shrug us off from a distance. He took up with her and her litter and left us to fend for ourselves.

My mother did the best she could. She gave us milk as we yelped and whined at her feet. She scavenged the dumpsters for leftover pizza crusts, we ate the chips left over at the bottom of the bag, we collected water from the fresh snow falls. My siblings and I found ways to occupy ourselves. We'd play cat and mouse with the other neighborhood kids, chasing each other through the alley ways and strangers' backyards. We learned how to hook our feet through the drain pipes and scale up the sides of the red brick apartment buildings. From the roofs of those buildings, the city stretched before us like tiny fireflies against the the black winter sky.

The millions of orange lights glimmering in the darkness reminding us that though we were small, we were not alone. We played in the streets late at night, dodging under parked cars to avoid the traffic. When you had no real home to go to, it was hard for my mother to enforce a curfew.

"You need to go out on your own, I'm pregnant again and can't take care of all of you", my mother said one morning, sitting on the dumpster behind the bagel shop. On Friday mornings they dumped leftover bagels from the day before, the ones that we're too stale to sell on the discount rack. We ate there every Friday morning, sometimes lucky enough to find bits of cream cheese or butter leftover on waxy paper wrappers from people littering.

"Where am I supposed to go?"

"You can go anywhere, I guess. You're old enough to take care of yourself, you're not a runt anymore. You're smart, you're scrappy. You'll figure something out." She rubbed her cheek lightly against mine and whispered, "Good luck out there, I'll be thinking about you."

She left me sitting on the dumpster alone. As she walked away some of the neighbor kids ran down the storm drain, following after her. "Tough break, Frank!", one of them yelled and disappeared down the alley. I finished the stale bagels, at least now I didn't have to share, and wondered what my next move would be. I guess she was right, I could go anywhere I wanted to now.

The winter was starting to let up some, the snow had stopped and the ice would be shrinking. The whole city dripped and woke up from its hibernation. You could start to smell the sun in the air again, the bitterness giving way to a clean spring. There would be more food in the springtime, people would be more generous. Maybe I could find some nice people in the neighborhood to help me out, maybe this wouldn't be so bad.

I climbed the fire escape of a small pink plastered building on St. John street. The place had been abandoned when the plumbing stopped working a few winters ago. The pipes froze up, the windows cracked and broken from the cold, leaving it unlivable.

The city condemned it and with the crippling years we've been having, no one wanted to make the investment in fixing it up. I climbed through the window and found one of the apartments had been left behind, still half furnished. The navy upholstered couch had seen some better days.

It was covered in old cigarette burns and the pillows had been ripped open where some birds had made a nest from their stuffing inside the radiator. The cold linoleum floor had aged a gross phlegm yellow color and the once white curtains were frayed. I tore the curtains down and wrapped them into a ball on the old couch. I curled myself up under them and had the best sleep of my life. This place was abandoned just like me and finally, I was home.

I lived in the apartment on St. John Street for three years. Some of the neighborhood kids I had grown up with moved in the apartments down the hall and upstairs. We created a new family in the pink building, being pushed out by ours. Everyone had the same story. New siblings had come along, mom had found a new man, the family moved deeper into the city where food was easier to come by but kindness wasn't. For one reason or another, we all had stuck around this part of town and found each other again on St. John Street. We shared what we had. The boys upstairs had found the best houses around the block to hit up for a free dinner.

Friendly neighbors, much better off that us, who left offerings of water and bowls of bland food on their front porches. Being just kids, once in awhile someone got lucky enough and cozied themselves up to a family to take them in, give them a place to stay. For my kind, that wasn't going to happen. I was set in my ways, not the most friendly or cozy guy around. I was affectionate sure, but it was on my terms and thats not the kind of stray a family would take in.

Four winters had gone by when someone finally bought the building. Development in the city had started to boom and the downtown area was spreading rapidly, our little neighborhood had held on for a long time but with more people moving into the area everyday, people grew desperate to buy up property.

Most of everyone moved themselves out of the building and back onto the streets.

Some were lucky enough to get taken in by others, some refused to move until they were forced out. Having nowhere to go, I stuck around until a large man dressed in black, with a low soft voice, showed up. He approached me slowly and promised a life better than this one.

He promised a place I could stay where it was warm, I would be fed and could spend my days hanging around with others like me. He had started a place for us a few miles away and said me and anyone else still is the building could join him. We made him promise we would all go together and he allowed me my old frayed curtains, the first thing to bring me comfort when I moved in years ago.

The place was everything he had promised. We still slept on worn linoleum floors, but the building had heat and he made sure we had at least two full meals everyday. It didn't look like much from the outside but it sat on 3 acres of green land just on the outskirts of the city. I could sit in the bay windows all day and watch the sky change, listen to the birds chirp, chase them across the grass with my eyes. There were lots of us there, even some friends I hadn't seen since my dumpster days.

It seemed like things were never going to get better than this, and for a long time they didn't. It had been about a year of dreaming in that bay window when they showed up. I saw them, a young couple, pull into the gravel driveway and slam the doors shut. It was winter again and they moved like black dots across the grey landscape. I heard them just outside my door, speaking to the man in hushed but excited tones.

For once I thought, maybe this would be it, maybe this would be my ticket out. They came into the room with the same hesitant and kind eyes that first rescued me from St. John Street. Sitting quietly in my bay window, the girl reached out and scratched behind my ears. The boy sat next to her, he smelled familiar, like something I knew, something safe. I hopped into his lap and he laughed a full, deep laugh. "I guess he chose us", he said to the girl and she smiled and nodded. "How would you like to come home with us, buddy? How would you like the name Frank?"

Life has never been better. I have cool, fresh water to drink when I want - my bowl is never empty. I sleep on couches, at the foot of the bed, sometimes in the bay window but now with a much different view. They scratch behind my ears and under my chin and when I've had enough I push their hands away. I get all the affection I could want, always on my terms, when I'm done I just push their hands away. The tuna treats are much better than any wax paper cream cheese. I know I'm one of the lucky ones and there's more out there, just like me. I've found my forever home and I'm not leaving.

Untitled

He pushes the hair back from my eyes
and says so sweetly, "I've been waiting
for this, for you."

I choke on my breath and try not to
laugh. Bring me back; bring me back
to Zen New Jersey.

I've been waiting for the heat in my car
to start up and for my adult interests to
form and for them to make peanut
butter Oreos. "Do they make peanut
butter Oreos?"

I was aiming for platonic
conversationalist. I was only looking
for intoxication and the occasional
good, hearty laugh, and opiates, and
strong brewed tea.

You're a cannibal. You're the bad
side of 4am, the side I never liked.

You're poetry and I'm drinking too
much these days. You are safe and
I am not safe
from blood, sweat, tears, and stale
shampoo pillows.

I've got a devil and an angel and
they're sitting on my shoulder and
I'm keeping you a secret from both of
them.

"...a soul to conform to the
rhythm of thought in his naked,
endless head."

I am more that a ghost. I am the
preacher, the choir, and the
congregation.

I am first and foremost, not making love
here. We are not making love, we are
making inspiration, can't you see?
Can you see the strewn
remnants of silk and of orange
and banana and of millions of
tiny yellow post its?

33

There's great success in throwing your
tampons out the window and crying
with the masses. He's saffron and
nutmeg and pure brown can sugar.
He's limestone and velvet curtains and I
am iceberg lettuce. Bring me back to the
mountains.

Dennis Greeno frequently visualizes taking another fork in the road after a long career in public accounting. Formed in 1989, the Goodlettsville, Tennessee. The CPA firm of Greeno CPA specializes in small business accounting, individual business tax compliance, business valuations, and fraud forensics.

His interest in literature started while he was stationed in England from 1975 to 1978 at the U.S. Air Force base formerly known as RAF Chicksands. Numerous day trips to London resulted in the acquisition of antique books, Penguin paperbacks, and the occasional Times Literary Supplement. An Air Force buddy introduced him to books by Kafka, Kerouac, and Vonnegut.

After the Air Force, he was an English major at Purdue University for two years. In 1980, in the midst of a jobless recession and double digit interest rates, he took the fork in the road leading to a degree in Accounting at Western Kentucky University.

Thanks to Amazon, Rhino Used Bookstore, and the Metro Library, he enjoys reading - especially poets such as W.S. Merwin, Hayden Carruth, and Seamus Heaney. A recent summer writing class led by Kemi Elufiede reignited his interest in creative writing for pleasure.

Trapped

I dreamed you came home from work
and I showed you the dead mouse in the
trap. You screamed and ran into the
bedroom where you opened the closet door
and you found your robe draped over
my head, while I swayed and you saw bits
of cheese on my lips and the robe's belt
hanging stiff from my back.

You ran screaming into the kitchen
where I poured you some coffee,
and I told you about Andy's pet mouse
escaping from its cage last night
and apparently hiding in our closet.
You then scampered off under the cabinets
squeaking and clawing your way back to
work.

Frigidaire

Dream Diary: *Giant balls of dental floss bounce and tumble across the landfill like albino sagebrush*

Three years have passed and the contorted skeleton of a little girl shrugs a what-me-worry inside a listing Frigidaire.

Dream Diary: *Hey Verne! That's her picture on this here milk carton!*

Bits and pieces of daily lives
scattered about the barren wasteland of the public landfill. This Princess reigns o'er majestically encased in her rusty throne.

Dream Diary: *The night after I opened the Frigidaire.*

Early one sticky summer morning, all 5,812 dumpsters in this olfactory town became self-propelled caissons, rolling silently on the back surface streets and

38

hitting the main arteries, converging on
West End Avenue, leaking their syrupy ooze
like snail trails down Harding Road.

No one, not even Traffic Jim, spots this
trackless railroad of rubbish as it merges on
to Belle Meade Boulevard.

Then, one by one, like the June Taylor
Dancers, the dumpsters poured their
fermented guts on the immaculate lawns.
Moments before the rising sun and alarm
clock summon us to awake to another day
of converting the tangible and intangible
into sweet putrescence.

Approaching San Angelo

"30 MPH!" shouted the sign
just as the AM station died
moments after the man murmured the time

"2 AM" had said the man

cruised by buzzing yellow arches
while crickets crunch under tires
radiator hissed when stopped at flashing red
lights hovering hot cloud over hood
with soundtrack of radio static

"2 AM" had said the man

where is that man?

shifted into reverse & stomped the gas
turned off the radio the man screamed
"STOP! STOP! STOP!"
speedometer yelled "30 MPH!"

man in the mirror now closer than he
appears hit the brakes, got out, opened
hood saw the man and jumped in

For Amber, on Your Second Christmas

If this will be your earliest memory,
forget the story about the moocow.

On this page, I have written a message for
you to keep forever, folded up in a crevice
of your purse or in a box in your attic.

Perhaps today, you are now a young lady
having pulled this out to pass time on a bus
ride.

Maybe you shake your head and laugh out
loud at the idea of your father writing such
nonsense.

What am I now?
Banker? Lawyer?
Accountant? Stranger?

This minute your past to be, instantly our
present. you are cuddled up on my lap.
We had fun tonight hanging tinsel on the
Christmas tree.

You laughed and pranced and clapped and
danced with streaks of silver in your hands.
It would be beautiful if you remember it as I
will.

Young lady, if I have turned out to be a
Stranger, throw this scribble away
because when you cry as you do now,
the way you curl your wrists as you rub
your eyes makes you such a delicate babe.
I press you to my hairy face and tell you
about the moocow.

Chelsea Champion is a Nashville transplant from Upstate New York. She has been dabbling in creative writing since grade school and particularly enjoys writing short stories and poetry. When she's not writing, she stays active by hiking, kayaking, and playing women's tackle football with the Music City Mizfits.

Breathe

Breathe life into me
Set fire to my soul
Whisper me your wishes
Turn my dreams to gold

Breathe life into me
Lay with me til I wake
A sweet and tender harmony
Our two heartbeats shall make

Breathe life into me
Your love so true and bold
I remind you once again that
My heart is yours to hold

Carpe Diem

Bold and fearless,
They can't get near us.
The meek and passive,
They fear us.

It's clear as rain,
Bright as day,
Say what you want,
And mean what you say.

Pay no mind to the others,
And go your own way,
You don't need anyone to tell
you

Today is YOUR day.
SEIZE IT.

How to Write a Poem

I embark on this creative
adventure, my imagination the
vessel in which my dreams blast
off into space, into poetry.

I see two thousand stars or
more, I'm not sure,
And capture these luminous
butterflies with my net, my
perfect pen.

The Foreclosure: A Life Taken

A car bumped down the gravel drive, spewing a trail of thick, gray dust in its wake. Cody watched the vehicle make its way along the serpentine path until it finally careened to a stop at the front of the house. It was just about noon and the sun was beating down on the farm, causing a harsh glare to reflect off of the windshield. Even while squinting, Cody could barely make out the shadow of a human figure fumbling with something in the driver's seat.

Within a few moments, the door to the car opened and the shadowy figure gave way to a slender, middle-aged man in a navy-blue suit. He carried with him a briefcase and stiffly approached the door to the house, adjusting his suit jacket along the way.

Before the unknown man could ring the doorbell, Cody emerged onto the porch to greet him. He didn't much care for strangers in his home, anyhow.

"Afternoon, sir." Cody announced, tipping the brim of his tattered baseball cap. "What can I help you with?"

The visitor, seemingly caught off guard by Cody's prompt and unsolicited greeting, or perhaps just nervous of the encounter, didn't answer immediately. Rather, he began frantically digging around in his jacket pockets as if he'd lost something. After rifling through some papers secured at the front of his left breast, a look of relief flashed across the man's face as he pulled out what appeared to be the winning ticket. The man glanced at the paper for a moment before refolding it and finally addressing Cody.

"Hello, sir. Are you Mr. Cody Bennett?" The man asked.

Why you asking? Cody thought, but revised his response to be a bit politer.

"Yes sir, that's me," he responded in the affirmative, still not sure of the man's business there.

As if reading his mind, the man answered, "Well sir, my name is Edward Shelton and I am with Great Plains Savings and Loans. I'm here today to discuss with you some changes on your mortgage that have come up. I saw it more fitting to come out here and discuss it in person rather than over the phone."

An uneasy feeling swept over Cody.

This can't be good, he thought, before inviting Mr. Shelton inside.

The two men sat and talked for only twenty minutes. Driving nearly an hour and a half to pay a business client a twenty-minute visit didn't seem well worth the man's time, but after hearing the news, Cody didn't want him to stay any longer. Mr. Shelton insisted on talking further to help Cody "work things out" with the bank, but Cody respectfully and firmly asked him to leave. It's not often that one takes kindly to his entire existence being taken out from underneath him.

Cody watched the banker's car retreat back down the driveway until all he could see was a tiny black speck on the horizon.

Once the car was gone, he again looked over the letter given to him by the bank. Key phrases jumped out at him.

Failure to make payments.

Foreclosure.

Eviction.

Effective March 1st.

Thirty days. I have to pack up twenty-five years of my life and generations of hard work in thirty days, Cody mused. At a loss for words and with no viable solution in sight, Cody did the only thing he could think of when he was feeling this hopeless – sought out his father.

Mr. Dale Bennett was the man who started it all. Fifty years ago on this very land, he took on the task of converting his own father's rundown subsistence farm into a booming business. Whereas previous generations only sought to grow enough to feed the family, Dale expanded on this notion, constructing new out buildings, buying up surrounding land, and investing in the newest machinery until he became the largest crop grower in the county. Within fifteen years, he had control of hundreds of acres of wheat, corn, and soybean fields that put food on his table as well as the tables of thousands of Americans across the nation. These same fields financed a new home and put two children through college. It was because of Dale's influence that Cody returned work on the farm after graduation – he wanted to continue the family legacy that his father had forged.

The unfavorable economic climate and rise of commercial agriculture was not kind to Cody's efforts. Falling crop prices and increased competition made it harder and harder for smaller, family-run operations to survive, so the past several years Cody had barely kept his head above water. Yet he had always managed to pull through by the end of the year, and figured this year would be no different. But much of last year's harvest fell victim to the severe droughts and subsequent famine in the area, causing the farm to take a big financial hit. Even with autumn's final harvest, Cody wasn't able to bring in enough crops to pay the bills. And now it cost him the farm.

51

Cutting through the backyard and hopping over the fence, Cody made his way up the one and only hill on the property. A gently sloping wave of prairie grass swished in the light breeze and tickled Cody's legs as he walked past. Reaching the top of the hill, he paused and took a seat next to its only inhabitant: a wooden cross with a small pile of rocks at its base.

"Hi Dad," he murmured, lying back on the grass, looking skyward. "I just wanted to let you know that I'm sorry. I feel like I failed you and all that you've worked for. I gave it my all, I really tried. I hope you know that."

Cody quieted briefly while he wiped the lone tear escaping down his cheek. Overcome by deep despair, he left it at that. He continued to lie silently there on that hill, soothed by the company of his late father, remaining there until nearly sunset.
As the twilight began to creep in and a flood of vibrant colors saturated the skyline, Cody sat up and took in the sights around him. Up here, he felt on top of the world. Up here, the banks couldn't touch him. Up here, he still had his father. He sat and absorbed the views of his kingdom before him, for what would be one of the last times. Safe from all worldly harms and worries, they sat together, awaiting the first twinkle of starlight atop the grassy knoll, at peace.

Tango

Two trees intertwine
Arboreal tango on
A forest dance floor

James Currey is a native Nashvillian. He attended Tennessee Tech University and has been a Professional Civil Engineer for much of his life. Jim served in the US Air Force and retired in 2002. He currently works for the Tennessee Department of Transportation, where he manages airport projects. Jim is a lifelong learner who thoroughly enjoys reading.

Drones Fill the Skies

Like bugs filling the sky around a nocturnal lantern, drones have become a commonplace sight in the skies around Nashville. Have you ever wondered who was operating these miniature aircraft and why they have become so prolific?

You can thank the United States military for this latest aviation fascination. Drones in their basic configuration are helicopters without pilots on board. They primarily launch and recover from any open area. Pilots or operators can be stationed anywhere within radio control range.

The larger military drone versions were introduced during our wars in the Middle East to provide low risk observation of enemy troops, equipment and facilities. They typically operated above 5,000 feet and could remain aloft for tens of hours. As smaller, tactical equipment was developed, drones were designed to fly as low as a few hundred feet up to five thousand feet, as they relayed real time intelligence on battlefield conditions. As weaponry and tactics were developed to address conflict conditions, drones took on a more controversial mission as weapons delivery systems. To this day, they are considered an essential component of battlefield air superiority for our military operations.

It was only a matter of time until the use of drones migrated into our commercial and general aviation communities. Currently, unmanned aerial vehicles are used in numerous operations. Some of these include bridge and building inspection, livestock inventory, police surveillance and package delivery. However, the most common public images come from drone use are at sporting events.

Unfortunately, their expanded utilization has not come without growing pains. With their danger to manned aircraft operating in the same airspace, the Federal Aviation Administration quickly moved to regulate drone use. Unmanned Aircraft were to have been registered with the FAA no later than February 19, 2016. Local law enforcement agencies also discovered that they could pose a threat to personal privacy.

If you consider owning and operating a drone, there are several important things to remember:

1. Decide if you want to operate it for recreational or commercial use. Requirements for commercial use are more stringent.

2. It must be licensed with the FAA.

3. Always protect yourself with insurance as you would for any other activity that impacts the public.

4. Restrict the use of UAVs to public areas. Privacy and trespass issues could otherwise cause problems.

It seems that drones, UAVs or unmanned aircraft are here to stay; and their use will probably increase as

greater benefits are demonstrated. Keep your eyes to the heavens.

The Book

We never know what wonders await,
When first we open a bookish gate.

The pages bring to life a tale,
For those whom a literary ocean sail.
The past speaks across the years,
To gently whisper in our ears.

The journey may harbor work and
sweat,
Rewards will leave us no regret.

When we travel to the past,
On wings that take us to the last.
The truth a book speaks is dear,
And wipes away our very fear.

When at last we reach the end,
We cherish the act we did begin.

The Soldier

Flies are the scourge and curse of mankind. Those nasty little creatures and their transitional maggots feed off dead flesh. I bear witness to the pestilence that offers no relief and is the harbinger of battlefield casualties. As a soldier in the army, I am constantly in the company of flies and death. I know them all too well. War carries with it the most horrible of environments: heat, cold, rain, dust, drought, disease, hunger. And yes, flies.

A hole in the ground is my home and a rock is my pillow. It is here that I contemplate my fate. Will I live or will I die? Will I be reduced to a vegetable? Will I exit this campaign without even a scratch? Within the next few days I will know. During the evening hours before sunrise, I consider what fate brought me to this place of death and destruction, what compelling forces caused me to be placed in harm's way. Could it be divine intervention or is it mortal folly and frivolity?

This war is a just war because God is on our side. It must be true because our most holy men told us so. We perform God's work by depriving other men of their lives. Why must that be true? Is it God's will or man's interpretation of God's will? Our most holy men have said that the enemy worships no God--or is it that they have a different God, but a noble supreme spirit nonetheless? Do they have holy men

59

and are they also telling them that this is a just war because God is on their side? Perhaps we differ greatly in our beliefs or perhaps we have no differences. Perhaps both are right and wrong.

This war is a just war because we are fighting for our country. It must be true because our nation's leaders told us so. We have been told that the enemy is an animal and not capable of cultured thoughts, that its barbarism drives it to kill civilized men for no good reason. Or perhaps the enemy is a refined man with noble thoughts and articulate methods who is simply defending his way of life. And maybe the enemy's political leaders are telling him that we are barbaric people bent on destruction. Or just maybe we and the enemy are very much alike.

This war is a just war because we are fighting for our family. It must be true because our loved ones told us so. Would the enemy subjugate our peoples? Our community is telling us that the enemy loves no one except themselves and their despicable way of life. They kill their young and make blood sacrifices. Or perhaps they are just like us and long for peace and tranquility--they are just struggling to find the right way to get there.

This war is just because I am fighting for survival. It must be true because I am afraid to die. No sane person would be fearless unless they had a lust to perish. This purely visceral voice speaks to me with unstained clarity. The world around me is only alive in my brain, but birth and death are immutable constants of the universe. I lust for survival because I am afraid of the unknown.

My fate is upon me. It is an hour before sunrise, when the earth has not shuttered awake. The enemy is just over the hill and soon we will be engaged in mortal combat for the sake of what we believe or what we fear.

Suddenly, a young man appears before me. He is dressed similarly and perhaps at another time, he and I could become friends. But on this day, he is my enemy. Is he fighting for his God? Is fighting for his country? Is he fighting for his family and those he loves? Or in a base form, is he fighting for his mortality? The last of my days have been filled with discomfort, pain and suffering. All to be rewarded with death.

Oh, the enchanting sting of death. The mortal wound gushes my life force. I will never know the answers to my questions, only the fate which conflict holds for me. A soldier's life is all I'll ever know and all I will ever be.

Perhaps in the future, there will be no need for war. We will only know victory and defeat as an esoteric thought. There may come a time when we will have no need for conflict. Maybe we will outgrow the quest for armed conflict and the quarrelsome need to raise our hands and smite another human. But on this day I drift into the unknown universe that lies beyond.

Persian or Greek warrior, Battle of Thermopylae, 480 BC

Afghan or American warrior, American War in Afghanistan, 2001

Seeding the Stars

Act Two, Scene One

(A grass prairie with snowcapped mountains in the background. It is twilight and the moon is high in the sky. A light cool wind blows through the temperate air. Two men and three women sit around a campfire outside a series of tents. They are discussing what to do next.)

Jules: I know it's time that we make our decision.

Mary: Yes, and this is probably the most important decision that we will ever make.

DeMarcus: So this will chart our destiny forever.

Barbara: How can it come down to this one single decision?

Judy: We all know the problems with DNA replication. A diverse species is the best insurance we have for survival.

DeMarcus: Mathematically, it makes sense to separate into groups. With three women and only two men, we'll optimize our chances.

Mary: I know. It seems like a crap shoot but something must give. If one woman and one man

63

are left behind, do the two remaining women go with one man? Or do we leave two women and one man?

Jules: The remaining man and woman head on out and take their chances.

DeMarcus: This does leave us with a quandary. There is no perfect solution. One person gets sick or dies and the whole plan could fail.

(End scene. A second moon rises.)

Scene 2

Jules: It is time. We know that we can't return to earth. Its ability to support life died out five hundred years ago and we don't know if it has fully recovered.

Barbara: We know. If we stay here, we're living on the edge. One catastrophic event and we're all gone. There goes the last remnant of the human race.

Mary: Splitting up would increase our chances of survival given that one group stays here and the other travels to Land Home 16.

Judy: I suppose it's obvious that one woman needs to go with each group. But how about the men? Who goes with whom?

DeMarcus: Looks like we're down to drawing straws or rolling dice.

Jules: It's a cruel fate but better to act than face extinction.

Kelly Key is a sixth-grade teacher and a Virginia native who studied English at the University of Mary Washington. She has lived in Nashville for a little over a year now and she is still in awe of all the great things Middle Tennessee has to offer. She loves exploring local opportunities in music and the arts and she continues to enjoy sampling Nashville cuisine as an undercover, unpaid, self-proclaimed food critic. Kelly is thrilled to have had the chance to collaborate with this talented group of writers, and she hopes you thoroughly enjoy delving into the world of her stories.

A Potter's Tale

Sandra Stephens at the pottery wheel in her garage in Thaxton, VA

Southwest Virginia native Sandra Stephens discovered a hidden talent later in life. She had always appreciated Native American artifacts and handmade pottery, and around the time she retired from Kessler Refrigeration at the age of seventy, she started to seriously consider taking a pottery class herself.

67

"First, I found one in Bedford, but that teacher had a lot of illness in her family and she wasn't making half the classes, and it kind of disbanded," she said.

Soon after, she discovered the Brambleton Center, located in nearby Roanoke, VA. She began taking classes there in 2010 with her niece-in-law, Erin Foster, on Tuesday nights.

Stephens expressed that the most challenging part of making pottery has always been centering the clay on the wheel.

"What every potter will tell you – it's the centering. f you can't center your work, then nothing, you know, nothing turns out right and that's still - today, I'm still struggling with that."

She first learned to center smaller, one-pound pieces of clay. She can now work pretty seamlessly with five-to-six-pound pieces. Other potters she knows are working with eight-to-ten-pound pieces of clay. When making a larger piece, it's sometimes easier to start with a two-pound piece of clay and then add on another two-pound piece and keep building from there, she said.

"The biggest piece I've ever done, I did today," Stephens beamed. Today, she was working on making a casserole dish, using the slab method of pottery. In this method, potters build pieces by molding slabs of clay with their hands instead of using the potting wheel.

Typically, Stephens prefers working with the wheel. But there are ways to incorporate both methods. "You can throw a bottomless piece and just make the sides, let it dry enough so you can handle it, and do a slab piece for the bottom," she said.

Stephens expressed that she likes to work with different types of clay depending on the purpose of her piece. If she is going to make cups or bowls, she prefers working with porcelain or white stoneware, which are smoother and good for hand-painting designs. Brown clay, on the other hand, has more grit to it, and sometimes glazes turn out better on brown clay than other kinds. When she makes casserole dishes, Stephens usually works with brown clay.

Though Stephens lives and works in Virginia, one of the potters she most admires is a Nashville local – Danielle McDaniel, otherwise known as "The Clay Lady." Stephens first learned about McDaniel by coming across the potter's YouTube channel. When Stephens was first learning pottery techniques, she would watch McDaniel's videos and take notes on her pointers about centering and opening up the clay. Since then, Stephens has introduced other potter friends to McDaniel's work.

In Southwest Virginia, Stephens admires local potter Carlos Dowling, who lives in Roanoke but is originally from Bermuda. Stephens follows his work because of his impressive artistic vision and the creativity in his pieces.

Stephens has found her recent journey in pottery to be very rewarding. Over the last seven years, she has seen the most improvement in her ability to make "feet" for her bowls and to produce larger pieces. The most rewarding thing about making pottery is just working with the clay and seeing the magnificent things you can make from a simple ball of clay, said Stephens.

"As they say – the shape is already there, in the clay, and you just have to find it and bring it out," she said, roughly quoting a book she is currently reading: *The Soul in the Clay* by Nendo Tamashii.

Stephens has found a lot of selling success in her balloon bowls. She makes these pieces by forming clay around an inflated balloon, letting the clay harden, and popping and removing the balloon. The end result is an asymmetrical bowl, almost akin to a type of abstract art.

"Sometimes it's accidental, what you're proud of," Stephens said.. She likened the process of pottery to the famous quote from *Forrest Gump*, "You never know what you've going to get." While glazing can be a frustrating process because it's hard to predict how the end result will turn out,

Stephens has accepted that this unpredictability is part of the charm of the potting process.

Stephens is currently selling pieces at Goose Creek Studio and Olde Mill Primitives In Southwest Virginia. She sometimes participates in local craft shows, as well.

Achilles in Summer

Three Nashville Julys ago, I cut my heel
on something silly, like my own clumsy
razor and its navigational system.
Sidewinding soapy trails and slips.

And it had happened so many times before,
I didn't think much of it.

To tell the truth, I don't recall seeing
unblemished stems beneath my own waist
for quite some time now. Too many end-
corners, not enough round tables. Rope
burn and rug burn and dog-leash burn, too.

Though delicate peaches are often chosen in
metaphor to describe a woman's supple
skin, this woman wonders if it is because
they, too, are easily bruised. Falling off their
trees and lumbering about in the newness
of the world.

To him, this small laceration was nothing to
shake off. Meticulously, he placed a small

73

bandage over it, barely pressing against the tender skin.
Afraid of unleashing a sort of inner Paris against my own Achilles. Flinching when I flinched.

The concentration in his eyes matched that of a person playing that old game, *Operation*. Tweezing delicate bones without striking metal. Conducting electricity within his heart's four chambers. I could almost feel the pulse myself.

Holes

12:00:07 p.m.

I had signed the paperwork, and all was finished. Sweet, warm beads of sweat started gathering around my hairline. I turned around, pleading with my eyes to the others. They sternly shook their heads at me and I knew there was no turning back now.

They shut the little door behind me. Walls of glass separated anxiety from freedom, and I was on the anxious side. Trapped. An orange-haired older lady nudged me toward the single leather chair. Her red false nails jabbed the small of my back. I looked down and saw her pointy black leather cowgirl boots beneath me. Nothing about her was soft – she was etched all in sharp lines.
 "Go on," the others told me. "It will be over soon."

I bit down and felt the blood rush to meet my teeth at my lip's surface. I tried to think of happy thoughts – distractions, but all that came to mind were the lyrics to "Captain Jack," that old Billy Joel song. Irrelevant and frustrating.

12:00:49 p.m.

I sat down. Silent tears trickled down my face and I gripped the arms of the chair. My knuckles were white and shaky. My sweaty palms slid involuntarily down the arms of the chair. "Hold still," the others said, "or you'll make it worse."

I sat there for what felt like hours, breathing and trying to be still. I knew the time was drawing near me. *One one thousand, two one thousand*, I counted in my head. How many one-thousands until it would all be over?

The orange-haired lady approached me. I looked up into her eyes for sympathy but found none. Instead, she seemed amused by my fear. She flipped her hair and chomped down on the wadded bubble gum crammed into her right cheek. *Chew one thousand, chew one thousand*...her ominous gum smacking joined into the rhythm of my mind games.

12:01:58 p.m.

I started to zone out and then felt something wet against my neck. Hospital smells filled the air. Part of me wanted to vomit, to let out some sort of release, but I was too tense to even move.
Twelve one thousand.

I closed my eyes, and when I opened them, the orange-haired lady was holding a gun to my head. I gave a little jump in my seat but tried as hard as I could to stay still. I didn't want to move and mess things up, for I knew I could only go through with this once. I felt a tight squeeze on my hand from someone and I closed my eyes once more.
 "One. Two. Three," the lady counted.
Click.

I felt a sharp twinge of pain on the right side of my head – metal meeting flesh and then penetrating it.

"Once more," the lady instructed, as she moved over to my left side. The vomit wishes returned, soon followed again by the neck-wetness and hospital smell.
 "One. Two." *Click*.
A new surge of pain startled me. *B-boom. B-boom*. The throbbing echoed in my head.
 "You didn't count to three!" I complained.
 "Well, it's over now," the orange-haired lady smiled at me.

12:03:38 p.m.

When I finally opened my eyes, I was staring at my own reflection – a new one. One with redness in my ears, as well as new sparkles there. The orange-haired lady handed me a bottle.

"You'll need to clean them with this twice a day, and don't take the studs out for six weeks," she advised.

78

"Okay," I said, finally letting out a sheepish grin. I looked up at my friends who were standing next to me on the other side of the short glass wall.

"You did it!" they exclaimed.
"Yeah," I said softly, "I did." I reached up and touched the new stones in my earlobes. "Come on, you guys. Let's go."

12:06:02 p.m.

My friends and I walked away from the mall kiosk, away from the orange-haired lady. I survived.

Three Men Eating

Three men walked into
A soup shop.
"One Potato"
"Two."

The third ordered lentil.
They complained about
All women
And just one man –

"The man," I think they called him –
And they made him sound quite
Distasteful, judging by their slurp.

They dunked their bread and chewed
Him out, grumbling
In their three-piece suits.

Julie Kramer always loved writing, but was so busy working and raising a family that she put that passion on hold. Recently, she decided to take a creative writing class through Nashville Community Education and her passion was rekindled. Julie is the ELL Specialist with the Nashville Adult Literacy Council where she trains volunteer tutors to teach English to adult immigrants.

Love Lost

Dean Peterson had been working at J. A. Peters Hardware for as long as anybody could remember. I had been working there for ten years myself, though Dean was there several years before me. Mr. Peters owned the store for about forty years until he died and his widow sold it to the Yates family. J. A. Peters had such a great reputation, Mr. Yates decided to hang on to the name and keep all of the employees.

Dean was as reliable and predictable as the sun coming up in the morning and setting in the evening. Monday through Friday, the number four bus would stop in front of the store at 7:30 a.m. and Dean would step off the bus, open the door, and begin his day. The store didn't open until 9:00, but Dean's job was to keep the place stocked and cleaned and to help customers carry purchases to their cars if they needed assistance.

He might also need to fetch something from the stockroom if a customer needed something that wasn't displayed on the floor. Dean was a fixture and knew almost every customer by name. He'd greet them with a "morning, Mr. Thomas" or "afternoon, Miss Pickering." They liked that. As Knoxville grew and the big chain stores like Home Depot and Lowe's moved in, J. A. Peters kept its customers. The customers liked the small store, friendly service, and of course, Dean Peterson. At 4:00 p.m. Dean would gather his lunchbox and hat and head back to the bus stop to wait for bus number four.

In all that time I worked with Dean, we had only exchanged pleasantries. "Good morning, Dean. How's it going today?" I'd say. "Good. Thank you," he'd reply. He was always quick to help when asked with a "sure" or "no problem" and I never heard much else from him. He'd eat his lunch alone at the small table in the stockroom and had the same thing every day: a bologna sandwich, potato chips, and a Coke.

Even when I or another associate sat there with him, there was never a conversation. He liked to read magazines while he ate and so we all ate quietly too. We'd bring in our old magazines for Dean to read. After a thirty-minute break, he'd be back on the floor without a word, just like clockwork. Every day felt like the one before. I never heard him talk about anything at all. I wasn't sure he had a family or any friends. He never mentioned anything and all the people who stopped by the store to shop seemed like nothing more than customers to him.

I sometimes wondered where Dean lived and what his life was like. The rest of us in the store were so close-- we socialized, celebrated birthdays and other special occasions together. But Dean always politely declined the invitations. I'd worked with him for ten years and somehow knew nothing at all about him.

It never snows much in Knoxville, but when it does, the city is paralyzed. It doesn't take much to close the whole place down. Last February, we had a snowstorm for the record books. The weather forecasters predicted four inches and we received eight. Mr. Yates decided we needed to keep the store open so our customers could pick up supplies to weather the storm. In no time, our shelves were cleared of ice melt, shovels, batteries, and sleds.

Since we had run out of most of the essentials, Mr. Yates decided to close the store at three instead of four that day. We were all preparing to leave when it hit me that Dean was depending on the bus to get him home.

"Dean, I'd be happy to give you a ride," I told him as we were grabbing our bags."No thanks. I'll wait for the bus," he said.

My conscience would not let me just drive away, so I made an excuse and told him I had some paperwork to do and I needed to work a little longer. 4 p.m. came and went. 5 p.m. did too. There was no sign of the bus and the snow was piling up. Dean was standing in the store looking out the window waiting for the bus to pull up. I waited nearby with my bag. "Dean, you can't stay here all night. Please let me take you home."

With a defeated look, he said, "Okay." He directed me to his home on the south side of town. It was a run- down clapboard house that was about ten years overdue for a painting. The porch was being used as a storage area for all kinds of rejected junk. I quickly realized it was a boarding house.

"Dean, how many people live here?"

"About six or eight, depending on the week," he said. "Dean, my wife is out of town," I lied. "I'm going to have to get some dinner. Would you like to join me?"

He looked at me with that familiar defeated look and said, "Okay." Hoping I could actually find something open during this snowstorm, we pulled out of the driveway. We headed over to the main highway and Clifton's Diner appeared to be open, so we pulled in. We walked in, found a booth and settled in. "My treat," I said. I ordered the meatloaf with mashed potatoes and green beans. Dean ordered a cheeseburger.

We sat quietly for a few minutes after we placed our order. Soon the silence became awkward. "Dean, I know you're a private person," I said. "But we've worked together for ten years and I feel bad that I don't know anything about you at all."

Dean sat quietly for a moment, looking at me as if he was deciding if I could be trusted. After all, he had known me for ten years too and he didn't know anything about me either.

"I lost everything," he began. " I had a beautiful wife that I met while I was in the service. I was in boot camp at Fort Benning and we'd sometimes get weekend leave. A few buddies and I headed into town and decided to go to Delilah's one night. The first face I saw when I walked in was Grace's. She was the most beautiful girl I had ever seen and I couldn't keep my eyes off her.

My buddies and I ordered beers and I asked the waitress to send one over to Grace. I watched her receive it and giggle with her girlfriends. After several songs played on the jukebox, I got up the nerve to go over to ask her for a dance. Right then, I knew she was the one. We kept in touch by mail while I finished boot camp and was sent to Florida. We visited each other when we could, ended up eloping, and moved into married housing on the base. She was perfect."

"How did you lose her?" I asked. "A stupid mistake. It was all my fault."

"What happened?"

"I stayed in the military for several years and Grace and I moved around. We were very happy, just the two of us. We wanted to have children, but it just wasn't meant to be. I stayed in the military for six years and we settled in Nashville. She had some cousins over there so we thought that would be a good place to live. I was always good with my hands and could fix anything. We had a little money saved up and so we bought a little house. We decided we'd open a handyman shop in our house. Like I said, I could fix just about anything.

"Grace was so sweet and loved people so much, so she offered to help write up the tickets when people brought in their merchandise and to handle the customer service side of things. I'd keep up with the repairs and the financial part. I put flyers out around town and ran a little ad in the paper and started getting a few customers. They were happy and told their friends about me and our business became very successful. We didn't have much overhead so our profit was good. Grace and I loved working together. Sometimes, husbands and wives don't want to be together all the time, but we loved it. Everything was perfect."

Dean's eyes began to well up. "One morning about 2 a.m., I heard somebody rummaging through my house. I'm a light sleeper and any little noise wakes me up. I walked quietly into my shop and saw a man wearing a ski mask opening the drawers and rifling through everything. He saw me and pointed a gun at me and quietly told me if I opened my mouth, he'd kill me. I was frozen, in shock. He opened my top desk drawer and found all my cash, put it in his pocket and ran out the door. I immediately called the police and woke Grace up. She was hysterical. The police came and filed a report."

"Wow. That's scary. Did you ever recover the money?"

"I never did," Dean said. "That was the stupid mistake. I've always been scared to put my money in a bank and Grace had no idea I kept all the money at home. You hear these stories about how banks lose people's money and there is nothing you can do, so I thought I was on the safe side keeping it at home. I just didn't trust anybody with my money. The robber took everything I had, about $200,000 and some jewelry. Grace and I had nothing to live on and couldn't pay our bills. Our house ended up being foreclosed and we had to declare bankruptcy. We tried to start over again and just never got to where we were. She blamed me for everything and she was right in doing so. I was stupid to keep that money at home. After about a year of living hand to mouth, she left me. She moved down to Huntsville where she was raised. Last I heard, she married a guy she dated in high school. That was several years ago."

"I'm really sorry. That must have been hard. So why did you move to Knoxville?"

"I came to Knoxville for a clean break. I wanted to go to a place where nobody knew me and I could start my life over. I stayed in Nashville for a couple of years after Grace left me.   I was able to get a job at Home Depot, but the pay was minimum wage and I was having a rough time. I ended up joining a church over there and they really helped me a lot. I never was much of a church- goer, but I had nothing to lose and needed help, so I went there. I found some good people there and enjoyed the programs. I got involved with the Room in the Inn program at the church where we would let a group of about ten homeless men spend Monday nights at the church. We would cook dinner, provide clean clothes and toiletries for them, and give them a place to sleep. My job was just to talk to the men and sometimes we'd play cards or watch TV. There were a couple of guys who came to our church every week and I felt really bad for them. They kind of helped me take my mind off of my own problems. One night, one of the guys named John and I started talking. He began to share his life story.

"He lost his wife to cancer. They didn't have any health insurance and it was hard for him to find doctors who would help her. The sicker she got, the more desperate he became. His family did what they could to help, but he needed money. He told me he committed several robberies and the money he used from selling everything he stole was used to pay for his wife's cancer treatment. He eventually was caught and served time in prison. He had lost everything, he said. John's wife died while he was in prison. When he finally got out, he had nowhere to go and very little to his name. All he had were the clothes he was arrested in, his wedding ring, and a stop watch. I saw the ring on his hand and he pulled the stopwatch out of his pocket to show me. I was shocked to see it was my stop watch that my father had left me when he died. John was the person who had robbed me."

As Dean finished his story, he appeared relaxed with me, like a burden had been lifted off him. I had known this man for ten years, but had no idea of his suffering. I sat there staring at him for a moment with new eyes, quieted by his words.

"How did you react to the guy? Were you angry?" I asked.

"Well, yes. I was angry because I was human. But I didn't say anything to him about the watch. What would have been the point? We both lost it all. We both loved our wives and wanted to provide for them. We both made terrible decisions that cost us everything and we have to live with what we did. Sure, it was different for him. He stole from me. But knowing his wife suffered like that. And the desperation he felt to save her. I saw myself in that. My heart broke for him."

"But it was his fault," I said. "I mean, his fault for your wife leaving you."He looked at the ground. "I wonder if she would have left me anyway."

"Hmm," I said.

"But I enjoy working at the hardware store," he said. "And I have a room I can call my own."

"Yeah," I said, wanting to tell him he should come to our work socials, hang out with us more.

We sat there together, the sound of cars passing outside drowning out the noise in the restaurant. I tried to think of a story I could tell that could matter as much as what Dean had just told me. I rested my hands on the table, then put them together, one over the other.

"I'm ready to go home now, if you don't mind," Dean said. So we got up, I drove him back, and he thanked me as he left. I wondered if he would continue taking the bus everyday, or if maybe, we had broken the pattern. I wondered about the watch on John's wrist and stealing it back for Dean, wanting to change his story. But it wasn't my place. It was better to just let things be.

My Evil Boarder

My mother was a poet. She had Multiple Sclerosis and often wrote poems about her battle with the disease. I decided to take one of my favorite poems written by her and add to it by using the "poem for you" prompt. You'll see her poem first. This poem was written about 1987 and she died in 2005. I tried to write my poem using the English sonnet format.

I have an evil boarder who lives deep inside of me.
My tenant's vile and gruesome face, my friends and family do not see.

Downstairs he leases my whole body;
upstairs he rents my very soul.
Wreaking havoc in all my rooms is his cruel and pleasurable goal.

We've tried forcibly to remove him but he will not go away.

He only brings in me more furniture and
continues there to stay.

One day soon he'll be evicted and have no
recourse but to flee,
Because when science throws him out,
there'll be no room for him in me.

Carol Lazarus Winkler, 1987

Untitled

Get out. Go away. Why won't you leave?
You were not invited and don't belong here.
If you would just vacate, we'd have a
chance to grieve. Your torture is much
worse than the death we fear.

I pray for comfort but it doesn't come.
I look for solutions but there are none.
When will you move out so she can again
whole become? Only you can decide when
you are done.

Slowly, you take her life away.
Each single moment worse than the one
before. A peaceful deserved-end you do
delay. An unwelcome tenant to abhor.

Finally, you move out after thirty years you
stayed. The most unwelcome houseguest,
an intruder on to the next home you'll
invade.

Brenda North is a native of Nashville, Tennessee. She grew up during the era of segregation, but received the best public school education because her teachers set high expectations and demanded that students excel. It was during those years that her love for reading and writing developed. She has an adult daughter and two adopted daughters in elementary school.

"Bla" "Bla" "Bla"

Some of the characters are based on real people but their names and other information have been changed.

Characters:

Dekota, a talented, very pretty, precocious know-it-all; eight-year-old girl who lives with her single mother and two other sisters.

Navada, a talented, very pretty, somewhat shy seven-year-old girl who often whines like a five-year-old to gain attention.

Sarah, the 25-year-old daughter of Mary who is engaged but still lives at home.

Mary, a single mother of three daughters.

Mrs. Utopia, an elderly resident of the Germantown neighborhood who sits on her porch in her gown and housecoat and chews tobacco.

In 2017, having a conversation with an eight-year-old going on thirty and a seven-year-old going on five is quite a challenge. Especially when they don't want to give you any information. The exchange below is a good example.

The Madison family lives in the upscale Germantown neighborhood of Nashville, TN. The tightknit neighborhood is within walking distance of the Bi-Centennial Mall, the new Sounds baseball field and even the Nissan Stadium, if you don't mind walking two or three miles. Dekota and Navada are two of only four young girls in the neighborhood. Dekota is so gregarious, the girls spend a lot of time outdoors playing with the other girls and talking to neighbors, or "being nosey", as Sarah says.

Mary tries to hold a conversation with them whenever they come in from outside to make sure they are not being meddlesome or a nuisance in the neighborhood. Sometimes the conversation is difficult to decode.

101

Mary: Hi girls, what have you been doing. Where have you been?

Navada: Nothing. Nowhere.

Dekota: We've been where we always go, over to the two girls' house, walking down 5ᵗʰ street, around the corner to the fish market, and wherever. We haven't been doing nothing, as usual. What is there to do? Nothing! I'm so bored. My life is SOOO boring.

Navada: Yeah. Boring.

Mary: Well, you've been out for almost two hours. You must have been doing something fun and interesting.

Dekota: Mother, you ask the same thing every time we go outside. There is nothing interesting in this neighborhood, not even in this city. Nothing! I'm hungry.

Navada: I'm hungry too. Can I have a grilled cheese sandwich and some celery with Ranch dressing and some ice cream?

Mary: "I'll fix you both a snack. How are your friends? Did you play at their house or where did you go?"

Navada: Bla, bla, bla, bla, that's what they said. That's all they ever say, bla, bla, bla, bla. Anyway, Dekota is always talking, so they can never get a word in. When can I get my snack? I'm hungry.

Dekota: You're always hungry, you little rat. Mother, can I have a fried bologna sandwich and some ice cream?

Mary: Yes Dekota, I'll fix you a sandwich. Now tell me what happened in school today.

Dekota: Nothing Mother. Nothing interesting ever happens. School is boring. My life is so boring. (*Dekota begins to make up a song and sing.*) Boring, boring, my life is soooo, so, oh, oh, oh, soooo boring. (*She dances around dipping and swooning like Ginger Rogers while singing her song. Her moves match the ups and downs in her song.*)

103

Mother: Dekota, if you focus on singing and learning to play the piano while you sing, your life won't be so boring. You do a good job of making up songs and dances.

Navada: What about me? I sing good too.

Mother: Sweetheart, you sing very well. I just want to encourage your sister to do things so she won't be bored. What did you do that was interesting today?

Navada (_with enthusiasm_**)**: I was a star student and I got to have THREE recesses!

Mary: Well, did you learn anything today?

Dekota: Nope, nada, not a thing. I told you the best thing about school is lunch and recess. The only thing I learned at lunch was never to sit by Paul again. He stuck his French fries up his nose then offered me one. He's GROSS, double GROSS. The only thing I learned at recess was to stay away from Dude, at least that's what he calls himself. He tried to put mulch down my back when I was hanging on the monkey bar.

Mary: Did you report either of those things to your teacher?

Dekota: I tried but she told me to ignore Paul and stay clear of Dude. Can I eat now?

Mary: Yes. What did you learn today Navada?

Navada: Umm, the same thing as yesterday. I told you we were studying weather – rain, snow, and stuff like that. I didn't learn anything today. I learned that yesterday. Mother, do you know what Dekota said to that old lady that lives in the gray house? The one who sits on the porch in her gown and housecoat? She said how are you doing, you look like you feel better, your nose doesn't look so big today. The lady, Mrs. Utopia, said, you sassy little girl, I'm going to call your mother. Get out of here.

Mary: Dekota, why did you say those mean things to Mrs. Utopia? That was rude, crude, just mean. I don't like that behavior. Finish eating. You're going to apologize to Mrs. Utopia.

Dekota: Mother, I was being nice, not mean. She does have a big nose. I didn't mean anything by it.

Mary: How many times have I told you that you can't say everything that you think and you need to think about people's feelings? Suppose she told you, your ears don't look so elfish today. You know how you think your ears look pointed and some of your school friends have teased you about them. Let's go.

Mary, Dekota and Navada go to Mrs. Utopia's house. She was still on the porch in her gown and housecoat. Mrs. Utopia was chewing her tobacco as usual and had her spit can nearby. The children had never seen her chew and spit because she was careful to hide her can whenever other people came by. As Mary and the girls walked up, she slid her can behind her and pushed her tobacco to the side of her mouth.

Mary: Hello Mrs. Utopia, how are you today? My youngest daughter Navada told me that her sister Dekota said some mean things to you today and I brought her by to apologize. I don't accept rude and mean behavior from my girls. Okay Dekota, go ahead.

Dekota: Umm, Mrs. Utopia, I'm sorry, I didn't mean to hurt your feelings.

Mrs. Utopia: Little girl, Dekota is it? You don't want to spar with an old lady like me. I'm eighty-eight years old and have been playing the "dozens" for seventy some odd years. Suppose I told you "my nose may be big and I may be old but my ears are not small and pointy and a sight to behold." Or, I could have said, "my nose might be big but yo mama wears a wig." Haha. That don't feel so good, does it?

Dekota: No, it doesn't feel good but that's WAY cool. Could you teach me how to dozen? Can I stop by after school and learn? I could really put Dude and Paul in their place.

Mary, Navada, and Mrs. Utopia laugh.

Mrs. Utopia: Dekota, you can stop by after school but I'm not going to teach you how to play the dozens. That's a way of hurting people. Now I can teach you how to be proud and how to respond to people who say mean things to you. You kill them with kindness.

After talking a little longer, Mary and the girls go home.

Mary: Do you understand what Mrs. Utopia told you about being proud and about treating people nicely? Do you Navada?

Navada: I understand Mother. Of course, you know that I don't say mean things to people anyway. But I'm glad to know that I can kill those girls who are mean to me with kindness. Mother, what is kindness?

Mother tries to answer but is cut off by Dekota

Dekota: I understand perfectly but I don't know if I'm going to do it. I like to be mean to people who are mean to me, but I'm not going to say mean things to Mrs. Utopia again. Mother, did you know Mrs. Utopia had tobacco in her mouth? She tried to hide it but I saw it in her jaw. I know because that's what I do to my vitamins when I don't want to take them. I put them in my jaw until they melt or until I'm out of your sight and I can spit them out.

Navada: You always spit your vitamins out. That's why you're not healthy. That's why you can't do ten sit ups. Na, na, na, na, na.

Mary: Okay girls, stop the bickering. Navada, kindness is being thoughtful, nice, caring, and gentle. It's following the golden rule, you know, treating other people the way you want to be treated. And Dekota, you *are* going to be kind to others. If I hear of you being mean to anybody, you will get a punishment.

Dekota: "Oh Mother, you know I was just kidding. I'm going to be good."

Dekota went on talking as they walked back home. As Navada would say, she said, "Bla, bla, bla," and nobody could get a word in edgewise

When A 7-Year-old Prays

I couldn't get out of bed for two days. Every time I tried to raise my head above the level of my pillow, the room spun, and I felt dizzy and nauseated. When I got up to go to the bathroom, I fell. Thankfully it was on my bed the first time and a basket of clothes the second time.

My seven-year-old daughter came downstairs to tell me it was 7:00 am. I was supposed to go to a meeting at church and she and her sister would get to spend time with a new sitter-- a college student.

The college student "D" had promised my eight-year-old, who is strongly into makeup, that she could do her makeup. She can only use her play makeup at home but she's always trying to sneak out with some eye shadow or blush on. My seven-year-old just wanted to be around "D."

After waking, I found that I couldn't get up out of bed. I asked for water and my seven-year-old brought me some water which I soon threw up. Later, after eating some toast and drinking some tea, I tried to get up again but was unable. I threw up the tea and toast. My adult daughter thought I had Vertigo and checked out the symptoms on the Internet. It indeed seemed like it. I spent the day in the bed on Saturday, my seven-year-old checking on me every thirty minutes or so. Later that evening, I told her that Mommy was sick and would she please pray for me. She, with great sincerity, prayed, asking God to not let her Mommy fall and to help her stop throwing up and to feel better. Shortly after her prayer, I began to feel better and was able to eat some dinner and keep it down.

The Vertigo returned in full force on Sunday, but I was able to keep all the tea, coffee, water, my lunch, and dinner down. I finally called my Doctor who called in a prescription for the nausea and dizziness, and got an appointment with her on Monday. But the beginning of my healing was as a result of my seven-year old's sincere prayer to God asking Him to keep me from falling, to stop me from throwing up and to help me feel better. Thank God and thank my daughter who knew how to get a prayer through.

What?

What? What asks a lot of questions- some superficial, some simple, some esoteric, some probing. This word can elicit all kinds of answers: What are you doing? Nothing.

That's the standard answer of a child to his/her parents. What do you want? A happy Meal. An iPhone, a red car with a let-down top. $50 so I can buy some make-up.

So, it's what follows the word what that matters. What is this piece all about?

The Smiles Sisters

Once upon a time, in the fair city of Happyland, there was a family, the Smiles family, with two daughters who were clever, active, and a little on the naughty side. Happyland was a small town, close to the big city of Nashville, with one Elementary School, one Middle School and one High School.

The town had a population of about 10,000 people; almost everyone knew almost everyone else. The Smiles knew most people in their daughter's elementary school, and of course, everyone knew the two Smiles sisters. The two sisters – Big Sister and Baby Sister -- fought day in and day out at home.

Big Sister was the oldest by 12 months and 1 week and she rubbed it in Baby Sister's face. She was a natural born leader and loved to boss others around. Baby Sister was somewhat shy but refused to let Big

Sister boss her around. She often told her, "You're not the boss of me."

The sisters fought over everything – pencils, paper, erasers, time in the bathroom. To others, it looked like they loathed each other. In fact, the elder was constantly telling the younger, "I hate you. I wish I didn't have a baby sister." Baby Sister was the same height as the elder and wore a size larger shoe, causing tension between the two.

The fighting went on all day, after school until bedtime; on the weekends, after breakfast until bedtime. But strangely, by bedtime, the sisters became friends again. They even hugged before going to bed. The parents longed for bedtime so they could get a break from the constant bickering. One thing the sisters agreed on was how to vex their parents, especially their mother, Mommie. Mommie, an executive, was a by-the-rules book person at work but a pushover with her daughters.

School functions always presented opportunities for the girls to try something that would worry the parents. During one talent show, the girls sat up front in the auditorium with their friends, away from the parents. They decided that it would be fun for one of them to get lost in the school and scare Mommie. Big Sister's BFFs were brought in on the plan so that they wouldn't give anything away. The girls decided that Big Sister would get lost and Baby Sister would sound the alarm.

"Mommie, Big Sister is missing," said Baby Sister. "She went to the bathroom and now I can't find her."

"I'm sure she'll be back," Mommie said. "Give her time to use the bathroom. There may be a lot of people needing to use it. Go back to your seat. She'll be back soon."

Five minutes later Baby Sister was back, tapping on Mommie's shoulder making the same claim. This time Mommie got up and went with Baby Sister to find Big Sister. No one was in the bathroom. Everyone seemed to be in the auditorium watching the talent show.

" Maybe she went to the one upstairs, let's look," Mommie said. No one was in that one either. There wasn't even anyone in the hallway. Mommie was a little concerned and became worried when Baby Sister began to cry "my sister is lost."

By the time Mommie and Baby Sister got back downstairs to the auditorium, the talent show was ending and people were filing out. Mommie stood just outside the door so that she could look for Big Sister. She didn't see her anywhere. She asked some of the friends she was sitting with if they had seen her, if she had come back from the bathroom. No one noticed that she was gone, although two of the girls, her BFFs, had a smile on their faces.

Baby Sister said, "Maybe we should go to the office and dial 911 so they can find her," and began to wail in earnest, or so Mommie thought. A couple of teachers stopped to ask what was the matter.

Baby Sister wailed, "Big Sister is missing. She went to the bathroom and never came back. We have to call the police." Of course the teachers became concerned and gathered several girls to check all the bathrooms on all three floors. While Mommie went to the office to speak with the principal, Baby Sister remained behind and told the teachers and other girls that she and her sister were playing a joke on their mother.

Mommie asked the Principal to announce over the intercom that Big Sister's family was looking for her and she was to meet them at the hallway in front of the Auditorium. As Mommie walked back to the meeting place, Big Sister walked behind her.

"What are you doing, where are you going?" asked Big Sister.

Not looking around, Mommie answered with worry in her voice, "My daughter, Big Sister is missing."

Big Sister walked around her mother, laughing and stood in front of her. "It's me

Mommie. I was playing a joke on you. I'm not lost."

Mommie decided to turn the joke on her. She said, "No, my daughter is a lot taller than you, with brown eyes like yours, but she doesn't look anything like you. And she would never play a joke like this on her mother. My daughter is meeting me in the hallway in front of the Auditorium."

"No Mommie, it's me. Baby Sister and I were playing a joke on you."

When they got to the Auditorium, Baby Sister ran to her mother and sister and said, "Big Sister, you're saved. You're not lost anymore."

Mommie said, "Who are you? I don't know you. I've got to get home. I think my children have gone on and are waiting on me."

Both girls began to cry. "Mommie it's us Big Sister and Baby Sister. We're your children. Mommie, Mommie, don't leave us. We're sorry, we were only joking."

"Sorry, I don't know you girls," Mommie said as she started to leave. The girls began to cry in earnest. They thought their mother had really forgotten all about them.

As Mommie reached the door with the girls trailing close behind, she turned around and said, "GOTCHA!!!"

The girls dried their tears, hugged Mommie, and promised to never play a joke like that on her again.

Nashville Public School Snow Days

Snow days are greeted with glee on the part of teachers and students alike. Teachers get a free day of rest. Rest from giving instruction, grading papers, lunchroom duty, bathroom supervision duty, dismissal duty and Monday morning meetings.

Teachers love snow days because they can sleep an extra hour or two, get that kitchen floor mopped, wash a load or two of clothes during daytime hours rather than 10pm at night, and spend time with their own children, or the love of their life, without falling asleep. Children love snow days because they get to play outside in the snow. If there's enough snow-- at least an inch-- they can make snow angels or have a snowball fight. On those rare occasions when Nashville gets two or more inches, they build snowmen.

121

Metro Nashville Public School's way of deciding snow days is quite interesting. If the snow forecast is for Clarksville, Montgomery County, which is at least 60 miles away, the Director will close Nashville Schools, even though there is no forecast for Nashville, Davidson County. However, if snow is predicted for Franklin, Williamson County, which is 15 miles away, the schools remain open. The rationale is that Clarksville is North of Nashville and bad weather always comes from the North; however, bad weather in Nashville usually comes from the West. The meteorologists on Channels 2, 4, and 5 say "If it's snowing in Jackson, which is west of Nashville, at 10 am, it will be in Nashville by 2 pm."

On the last snow day in January, the weather stations predicted snow with an accumulation of half an inch to one inch of snow in the areas closest to Nashville and possibly in Nashville. What did MNPS do? They called schools open but had to close early due to snow and slick roads. Sometimes it's hard to predict when snow will hit in Nashville.

Leaving Dallas

Making the most money I ever had in my career,

With the executive position that to me was so dear,

I moved over 600 miles with great expectations,

But less than two years later lived day to day in consternation.

Having been told all my years I was a quick learner, I couldn't

Understand why things wouldn't

Come together in my mind, in my heart, for this job, no career

That I held so dear.

But after driving over twenty hours home and back eight times in a year,

I decided to look really hard at this career that I held so dear.

So with introspection and truth telling I realized that it just wasn't a good fit

Because money won't make you happy if what you do daily, your heart isn't in it.

So, I talked to my boss, gave my notice, worked out a severance package,

Hired a moving company and turned the page.

Back home to Nashville, a place that I love, with friends and family

That I only have to drive 15 to 30 minutes to see

I realized that the problem wasn't Dallas, It was me.

Denise Sheehan has been a Nashville resident for more than 30 years. She has written copy, bios and press releases as a part of her profession. She has recently begun to explore other types of writing.

Competitive Edge

The day Joe McIver moved into the Hillcrest Acres' assisted living community, you could feel the excitement among the female residents. He considerably upped the ante— at ninety-seven, he was fully mobile (except for a cane), well-dressed, freshly shaven and smiling. While the staff felt a fresh breeze when he entered, the residents felt their temperature rise.

The women, sometimes just one and other times in groups of two or three, tried to engage him in conversation passing in the hall or at meal times. He was unfailingly polite, but standoffish. The men didn't have much more luck--maybe a brief conversation about his previous work life, but he wasn't very forthcoming. He never divulged his age, even when asked directly. Because his mysterious aura, there was plenty of room for speculation. The residents often whispered among each other when he passed by.

The one time Joe relaxed was when he was walking. He loved strolling the grounds and beyond into the beautifully groomed campus of Furman University. The climate in Greenville, South Carolina was warm enough to suit him without the oppressive heat of south Florida, and he loved experiencing different seasons. He walked the paved path that wound around the perimeter of the campus, settling in to the lovely air.

Rose Pennell had lived at Hillcrest for almost five years. She had seen her share of folks coming and going, sometimes leaving to return to their homes or move in with family, sometimes a more celestial move. She watched Joe leave each morning and afternoon on his walks. She noted the direction he took and how long he'd be gone. On a Friday, she made her move, heading out a few minutes before his usual starting time in the direction he always traveled. After about a quarter of a mile, she stopped ostensibly to look the blooming peonies. She returned to the path just as

127

Joe passed. "Oh, hi Joe, we met at dinner the other night—I'm Rose," she said. "Have you seen these gorgeous peonies? They smell divine."

Joe paused to look at the flowers and the woman. She looked vaguely familiar and was nice and trim just like his wife, Cricket. As soon as he thought of Cricket, he felt a pang of guilt, as if just by being polite to a woman, he was cheating on her. He had always assumed he would die first—that was the natural order of things, but life didn't play out that way for them, despite their strong faith. They lost a son twenty years ago in an accident, and then Cricket passed after 73 years of marriage.

With a start, Joe realized that once again he was going down the proverbial memory lane. He dragged himself back to the present, realizing that he'd been rude to Rose. He shook his head and said apologetically, "Sorry, Rose, you caught me reminiscing. I hadn't even noticed the flowers, but they are lovely. I'm usually watching the students-- I enjoy seeing these young people moving about which such purpose."

Joe resumed walking—he usually walked about a mile, but today he was planning on going farther—and noticed Rose keeping pace with him. "Mind if I tag along?" she asked. "It's nice to have company—sometimes I'm not so sure of footing."

"I guess that's fine, if you want," Joe responded, though he preferred to be alone. As they walked on, Joe was glad that Rose wasn't one of those women who constantly had to be talking. He turned to head back at the usual spot, forgoing his plans for a longer walk. As they approached Hillcrest, he stopped at the rocking chairs outside, as was his habit, pulling up a chair. Rose played it cool and continued inside with a little wave. She knew the word would get out quickly that she was making time with Joe and that made her smile. She'd always had a competitive edge.

Happily Ever After

Dog wants in, dog wants out.
Barking, whining,

a ceaseless battle for attention.

It wears on my nerves, makes me
regret being seduced by cuteness,
affection, the idea of a faithful
companion.

Like picking the wrong spouse,
only harder to get rid of.

Silent Runnings

I watched a raindrop
slip down the center vein of a
magnolia leaf, starting slowly,
gathering speed. It slid off the tip
only to be replaced by another.

It could have been a tear,
silently traveling her red and
swollen cheek.
A salty reminder of pain and
humiliation starting a flood of
shame.

Steven Sheehan, a Massachusetts native, has lived in Nashville since 1983. He has spent thirty years in the music business as a musician, producer and songwriter. His songs have been recorded by artists in multiple genres in the US and Europe. This year was his first try at writing outside the format of commercial songwriting.

Sputnik!

Sitting in the saddle, helmet strapped tight, he pumped his leg muscles and felt the therapeutic rush of an early morning ride. Eleven miles from home, he began climbing a trio of peaks, the last and highest of the three felt like hell on wheels due to it's steep vertical ascent.

He stood out of the saddle and attacked the last quarter mile like a man possessed, fist pumping the alpine air as he reached the summit. From that point it was all downhill. He immediately increased his speed in full tuck position as he descended the remote mountain road. The dense aromatic forest of spruce trees lined the road 's edges like sentinels guiding him in flight.

Jason could never have imagined that in a split second his fifty-two year old body would intersect with the trajectory of a one hundred twenty-five pound white tailed buck as his bike reached a top speed of thirty eight miles an hour.

The deer, innocent of any wrongdoing had simply jumped out of the woods. Unharmed and unfazed, he disappeared back into the trees without any apparent injury.

Jason, on the other hand, lay in a mangled heap below his bike in the middle of the road. Semi-conscious, and unaware as to the extent of his own injuries, he eventually felt himself being lifted up into orbit just like one of his satellites. He needed to phone Estelle. He wanted to tell her all about it.

Summer Snow

Drifting across the great plains of stained hardwood accumulating in the perfect geometric corners of our living room

The slightest breeze from an open window like a chinook, paints a fresh white blanket atop the persian in the hall

Swirling and dancing, inching its way into the deep recesses of the kitchen pantry like a great glacial expanse bristling under the illumination of a single recessed halogen bulb

We can easily forecast the daily silent tempest with a minimum of meteorological skill

The inevitable deep sweeping effects however are better tolerated with the aid of a tumbler of iced bourbon or, an anxiety reducing pill

Our family's pet who's name is luna, relaxes on her plush cushioned bed beside the ac vent in the den

The corners of her lips often curl along the uneven edges of her teeth like a devious smile while she pants lying in cool comfort from the extreme heat outdoors

I often look at her and wonder if in her canine slumber she ever dreams of the changing seasons and secretly laughs about the impending blizzard of winter

Louan Tillman is a native of Nashville and owns a small business engaged in engineered solutions for Stormwater management. She loves to travel and has recently visited Iceland to see the Northern Lights, the Taj Mahal in India, and Mexico to swim with whale sharks just to name a few adventures. She took this writing class as a lark because it sounded like fun and is thrilled to be involved with the publication of some of the class works.

My First

I've never written a poem before.
It's such a daunting task.
Seeking form and inspiration,
I wondered who to ask.

Google, the web, and friends across the
nation. All willing to share advice.
Be epic, heartfelt, or silly they said
Or perhaps an ode to mice

The poem is due on Sunday.
I'm running out of time.
One thing now very clear to me,
Not all words have to rhyme.

My first is now in the past.
And nothing left to do.
Knowledge in place and time on my hands.
I'm starting number two.

Hope

Hope, a rambunctious, curious child, lived in a bubble. An airtight, reflective bubble that wrapped around planet Earth, making the surface dark and gray. In the years after the discovery of the hole in the ozone layer, the leaders decided the only way to save the planet was to wrap it in the bubble to keep the sun from burning up all that was left alive on earth. The plants and trees had died off years ago. The animals were all gone too. The surface of the earth was as barren as a desert. Nothing but waves and waves of blistered earth dried to sand and darkened by the shade of the bubble that was keeping the people alive.

The people lived underground, where the temperature was a moderate 98 degrees during the day and only slightly cooler at night. They got used to it. They had to. It was the only way to survive. Even with the bubble the topside temperature was over 150 degrees during the light hours, and nobody could stand that for long. To survive, the people carved into the ground and through the rocks and built a city like an ant colony, with tunnels for the roads, and living area cubbies branching off like cul-de-sacs in one of the old topside neighborhoods. In the tunnels, the focus was on work, every task designed to help them survive.

Cleaning the air with air scrubbers, making the recycled water safe to drink, and growing what food they could using an elaborate lighting system originally designed for growing marijuana in a closet back in the day. The hybrid food seeds had been salvaged from the doomsday vault in Norway when it became clear that the remaining citizens of the world would have to go underground.

Thank God someone had the foresight to save food seeds. Otherwise everyone would have starved years ago. The vault had modified seeds, equipment, and tools -- all the essentials man would need to make food and water to survive the catastrophe. But in the plan to save humanity no one thought to save the essence of what made them human. No one raced to grab the art they so admired or the books that shaped their discourse and provoked thought.

No one thought to bring the sixty-four pack of Crayola crayons so the next generations would know all the colors, or to bring rose cuttings, so they could grow them in their new home and the people of the future would know the beauty of that smell. No photographs of long-ago families or reminders of life before the bubble. There were no pictures to brighten the walls and no color in this gray place. There was nothing to remind them of the smiles and laughter that had existed before life underground in the gray. No beauty, no color, no joy.

After a while, people forgot such things ever existed. Generations grew up knowing only the work of survival and the gray of their world. In this dark place, the workers marched out each day in their gray uniforms, down the gray tunnels, traveling to their workstations where they performed tasks with robot-like precision. After their shifts, they went back to the holes cut in the rocks that they now called home. This is the world that Hope was born into. She never knew the green of the trees or the red of the tulips. She never wondered at the beauty of a star-filled sky or played in the light of a full moon. She was one of only a few young girls living in the tunnels, so her parents were overprotective of her, one working a day shift and the other at night so she was rarely left alone. When she was young she spent long hours in the cubby with one parent or the other sleeping off a long day of work. Schools had disbanded long ago when no one could remember the point of having them. Why educate the young when the future was so bleak and held only work for survival? Repetitive tasks worked better with a mindless population. Don't teach them to think. Don't teach them to ask questions. Don't wonder. Just do.

As a child, Hope was content with the arrangement; because the tunnels were dark, scary places, she felt safe in her home carved in the stone. But as Hope grew up, she began to wonder about the world outside the tunnels that no one ever wanted to talk about. When she turned twelve, she decided she was old enough to venture out of her cubby. One evening when the night grew still and Poppy was snoring, she snuck out to explore. She only went a short distance the first night but as her courage grew she began going further and further into the tunnels.

One night after months of secret trips and hiding in the crevices to avoid detection, she found herself at the entrance to a tunnel that lead topside. Did she dare step out of the safety of the tunnels? Night after night she returned to the same point, wrestling with the choice to stay in the tunnel or venture out for a peek. After months of indecision, her curiosity got the better of her and she stepped out onto the sand. Vowing not to stay long, she began her exploration.

Walking in circles around the opening to the tunnel, she made one loop, then another and another in ever-widening circles, then came upon a pile of rocks. Curious like any twelve-year-old would be, she began climbing on the rocks to see what she could see. As she climbed over the first pile of rocks she found a small open space barely as large as the family's weekly food bucket. There in the space was something she had never seen before.

She had no words to describe it. If anyone had saved the crayons all those many years before, perhaps she would have recognized the leaves as a pine green color and the flower as razzmatazz purple. A reference book would have called it Ipomoea turbinata or the purple moonflower but she had no way to know any of that. She only knew that it was beautiful, with the petals like arms spreading wide, reaching high toward the heavens. It was her secret. She couldn't tell anybody because she wasn't supposed to be there.

"Never leave the tunnel" was the mantra she heard day and night. Yet here she was out on the sand and nothing bad had happened. Just the opposite, really. She had made a wonderful discovery. She found color and a new living thing and it made her smile--something she didn't even know she could do. After gazing at this newfound wonder for a while, she realized that she had been gone way too long.

She hurriedly raced back toward the entrance and into the tunnels running full speed back to her cubby where her Poppy was just starting to stir. She dove into bed and pretended to be asleep when he stuck his head in to wake her for the day. Mums came home from her shift and immediately went to bed just as Poppy left for his shift. Hope was left alone with the thoughts of her daring and the discovery. All that day she tried not to smile but she couldn't contain herself.

She was glad no one was around to see. She was sure they would think her touched in the head and lock her away. People in the tunnels didn't smile at all. Especially for no reason. But she had a reason. She had a secret. A wonderful, beautiful secret, she couldn't wait for nightfall when she planned to sneak out again to her special place and gaze upon the beauty she'd found. Poppy came in after work just the same as every other evening and went straight to bed as Mums rushed out the door for her shift.

As soon as Hope was sure the coast was clear and the night noises had quieted off she went heading straight for the tunnel entrance. She dashed out onto the sand and hopped onto the rocks with anticipation, but something was wrong. There were three boys there in her secret place. One was holding her secret he had pulled up from the sand. She had not yet given it a name and she had never even heard the word flower. She only knew that it was hers and it no longer was spread open to the heavens but closed up like a pod. The beautiful colors were fast fading as her secret was wilting in the heat and near death. She screamed at them "What have you done?" but they only looked away.

She sprang into the middle of the three pushing them aside like a madwoman and grabbing for her secret. They dropped it and scampered away, yelling back that they had followed her the night before and watched her leave the tunnel. Since nobody ever left the tunnel they came back to investigate and discovered her secret. They pulled it up from the sand to take it into the tunnel not realizing it would die. No words they could muster would ever explain. They left her on the sand with tears streaming down her face.

She tried to put her secret back in the ground and coax it back to life but nothing she could do would save it. She sat there in tears until she noticed how late it had become and that she needed to get back. Dejectedly she made her way back into the tunnel and back to the cubby where Poppy was stirring preparing to start his day. Again, she pretended sleep as he dashed out the door, passing Mums coming in like ships in the night.

Hope stayed in bed all that day and most of the next. In fact, she barely stirred for nearly a month. Poppy thought she might not be well and offered to take her to the clinic but she refused, saying she was just tired and needed to rest. After a month or so of moping around the cubby she knew it was time to move on and get out again. Perhaps it was all just a dream anyway and not even real, she thought. How could something so beautiful survive in a world without beauty? How could those colors exist in the gray world they now called home? Even as she asked herself those questions she knew she had experienced something special, and whether real or a dream, it did not matter.

To make sure she would remember all the details, she decided to give her secret a name. In the future when it happened across her memory she would call it Joy and remember the way it made her feel. When she thought of the bright colors and the beauty of the open petals, or to her, "arms," reaching toward the heavens on the other side of the bubble, it always made her smile. Real or not it was still her secret. Her secret Joy. And every now and again she would sneak out at night to her place in the rocks and remember.

Years passed. The rocks became known as the rocks of Hope by the tunnel dwellers as rumors of her adventure spread. "The place where her secret joy once lived" they repeated to each other even though none of them believed a word of the story. There could be no color or beauty in this dark gray place.

Yet one night another young girl, another curious twelve-year-old, wandered from the tunnel and into the rocks to see for herself. She had heard the story for years and she had to know. She climbed up and over and into the sacred space and gasped. There it was. Ipomoea turbinata-the purple moonflower. She had found Joy just where her mother Hope said she would. And for the first time ever she smiled.

WHALE SHARKS

See Them While You Still Can

 Whale sharks are the largest fish on earth and found primarily in warm tropical waters. In March of 2016, these beautiful creatures were placed on the endangered species list, suffering a 63% drop in population in the last 75 years. They were red listed by the International Union for Conservation of Nature because of threats to their habitat, commercial harvesting for their fins, and accidental vessel strikes.

Marine pollution events such as the oil spill from the Deepwater Horizon are cited as having an impact on the Atlantic population which now represents less than 25% of the total remaining global population.

It was this significant decline in population and their new endangered status that led me to take a trip to Mexico to see them for myself. "Extraordinary" is the best way I know to describe leaping into the open ocean with a pod of seven of these creatures we were lucky enough to find.

We were the first boat to happen upon them at the feeding grounds north of Isla Mujeres and our captain was kind enough not to call out to the other boats until our group had spent about an hour swimming with these slow moving, gentle giants.

We were instructed not to touch them, but apparently the whale sharks did not receive the same instructions as they routinely brushed up against us. Imagine the thrill of swimming side by side with a thirty-five foot long, twenty-one-ton fish with its five-foot mouth wide open enjoying lunch.

The whale shark is a filter feeder, feeding primarily on plankton, so they represent no threat to humans--which was good for me since I spent time face-to-face with one! After swimming with them, I can see why whale sharks are worshipped in Vietnamese culture as a deity and the Filipinos feature it on the 100-peso bill.

They are truly majestic, beautiful, massive, and magnificent, and climbing out of the water back onto the boat I knew I'd experienced an adventure to remember the rest of my life.

As we returned to the dock, I talked to our captain about the new laws being enacted In Mexico to limit the number of boats allowed to take divers to the whale shark feeding grounds. The fear is the disruption of habitat, causing an even greater reduction in population.

Some, like him, feel a responsibility to protect the whale sharks, so he chooses to cut back on the number of weekly tours he takes. With the diminishing whale shark population and the cut back on the number of available tours, fewer people will have the opportunity to witness first hand these amazing creatures in their native habitat. My advice? Go. You'll be so glad you did.

Mike Wargo is originally from Indiana. He is a writer based out of Nashville, TN. Often using his life as inspiration, Wargo's works have ranged from poetry to novels to feature films and he is constantly working on new projects to make his voice heard. At the time of publication, he is working on a follow-up screenplay to his award-winning feature film "Stage 5" and is drafting his first novel.

Barlights

The Boy hears the garage door close and slips down the two floors to the basement. He keeps his ears perked, leaving the basement door open to hear any sound of his parents' return. He sees his reflection in the mirror behind the bottles, lit up by the built-in shelf lights.

He steps toward the wall of bottles and tries to pick from the choices he knows nothing about. He grabs the square bottle with the black label that his father used to pour from while he tucked himself into bed as a child. This was between the second and third wife, neither of whom liked the Boy very much. This was while they shared a one-bedroom apartment for two years.

The Boy fills half a tumbler with the whiskey, not bothering to emulate his father, who used ice. The Boy runs back upstairs once more to check the garage for his father's mini-van. He and his new son would be at the baseball diamond by now.

155

The Boy was not invited. He picks up the glass with a sense of trepidation and smells it. It sends a shiver down his spine. He spent a week building up the courage to take his first drink.

He looks at the posters around the room of all the men his father admired, each with a drink in his hand. Frank Sinatra, Sammy Davis Jr, and Dean Martin hang on one wall, laughing eternally with glasses in their hands. On the other wall, Humphrey Bogart says, "The whole world is three drinks behind." Bogie stares at the Boy as if to say, "Better catch up, kid."

The Boy takes a breath and swallows half of the drink in one gulp, trying not to taste it. He almost loses his balance as his body shivers and his head swims. His stomach and throat burns. His hands shake and some of the whiskey splashes on his fingers gripping the glass.

More than anything he wants to pour the whiskey back in the bottle. He spills some whiskey on the oak bar his father paid to have built and rethinks his plan of action.

He stares at the glass for a long while, as his stomach continues to churn. Without bracing himself, he accepts his fate and downs the rest of the whiskey in one quick swig, shuddering once again.

The Boy can't keep himself from falling as his legs shake under him and he lands with a thud. He stares up at the lights illuminating the bottles. He would get to know each bottle on those shelves better than any fifteen year old ever should. And they would become his only companions in the end. But, as is often the case, the Boy doesn't know this. He has no idea what those companions will give and what they will take from him as he fades away into sleep.

The Beach

You light up a joint and inhale.

You let the smoke flow through you,

caking your lungs.

You wrinkle your toes

and feel grains of sand sticking to the soles
of your feet

as you cough

and puffs of smoke pour from your mouth.

You clear your chest,

but still feel a burning, sticky sensation
lying against your ribs.

You take another drag and listen to the
waves crash.

You watch the moon hover over the water.

You feel a light breeze brush your face.

You can feel a small weight pulling on your eyelids.

You look to your left

and see a party down the beach.

Dancing silhouettes against a bonfire backlight.

They drink and you contemplate joining them.

But that's too far

and you just got comfortable.

You look to your right

and see seagulls picking at trash and food left behind by the beachgoers of the day.

You take another drag

and start to get hungry.

You salivate at the thought of a burger and shake from the restaurant down the beach.

But that's too far

and you just got comfortable.

You lie back on the sand

and feel the earth move to your body.

You take another hit

and let the weight pull your eyes shut.

You hear the tide rolling in and out

and hear the nearby bushes rattling against the wind.

You contemplate going home and getting into bed.

But that's too far

and you just got comfortable.

You feel the tide touch your heel and roll back out.

You could get up

but you take another hit and lie still.

The tide rolls over your ankle

and touches the hem of your jeans.

You suddenly start to feel the cold water crawl up your back.

You don't mind the water as it covers your chest

and the sand starts to sink underneath you.

The joint washes from your hand.

You contemplate chasing after it.

You drown.

You contemplate letting your soul go to heaven.

But that's too far and you just got comfortable.

He Asks Me

I sit staring at the generic beach painting on the wall, waiting. The doctor enters and sits behind his desk. I let him get started. He asks me if this is my first time in therapy.

"I spent a year with a woman in second grade. My parents split and they thought I needed help."

He asks me what I thought of it.

"It was a long time ago. I don't really remember much of it."

He asks me why I'm back after nearly twenty years.

"You want the honest answer?"

He says yes, of course.

"Drugs." He doesn't respond, waiting for me to continue. "I figure I've tried everything but that. Exercise. Yoga. Alcohol. Weed. None of it really helped."

The doctor refers to my chart for a moment. He asks how long I've felt depressed and anxious.

"Years," I say. "I had a lot of problems in high school. You know, not a lot of friends, picked on by the jocks, certainly no girlfriend. The usual cliché bullshit. I'd say it's been pretty consistently bad since then." He takes notes in his pad while I talk. "It kind of just went on and on for going on uhhhh... ten years now? I mean I have good days, like everybody else. There just seems to be less and less these days."

He asks me why I think that is.

"I think it's got a lot to do with my girlfriend, to tell the truth. It's the weirdest thing. Like, from sophomore year of high school all the way up to when I met her, like three years ago in college, I was pretty consistently miserable. Like most days were bad days, but they were bearable, you know?

Like I was kind of numb to it at that point? And then I meet her and there are suddenly more good days. Like, out of nowhere. And once that started happening, the bad days got a lot worse on the days I had them because I wasn't completely numb to everything anymore. Like, "incapable of getting out of bed" bad. Like Brian Wilson bad. And that's been going on for a few years now."

He asks me about my parents.

"What about them?"

He asks if either of them experienced any similar issues.

"It's on the form I filled out in the waiting room."

He says he wants to hear me tell it.

"Well, let's see, my mom has been treated for anxiety and depression since before I was born. But she didn't start taking anything until she quit drinking when I was a baby. And my dad was diagnosed with depression after he and my mom split. I don't know if he still gets treated or not."

He asks me why I decided to seek out treatment on my own for the first time.

"I told you. I want drugs."

He says other than that. He asks why I want drugs after so many years of being untreated. "Really, I want to stop being a burden to my girlfriend. Whenever I have one of my really bad days, she has to drop everything and take care of me.

She has to cancel plans with friends. We had to leave a party she'd been looking forward to for months because my anxiety got so bad, I couldn't stop shaking. I need drugs because I'm afraid. I'm afraid if I don't get my shit together, she's gonna get tired of taking care of me. I can't keep asking her to start and stop her life because I can't keep it together for a few days." I'm crying now. "I need help. And believe me when I tell you that I don't ask for help. Ever. But I can't keep doing this on my own. I can't.

We sit in silence.

"...so, what am I supposed to do?"

He doesn't respond. He never does. Maybe a real psychiatrist would be able to answer me, not just the imagined doctor I talk to in the car on my way home. I stare down the bumper of the Kia in front of me. Maybe I should actually look into seeing a real doctor when I get home...
Maybe tomorrow...

167

What to Wear When a Loved One Goes Missing

So your wife/husband/child/parent has gone missing. It's a tough time and there's so much to do. You have to be interrogated to remove any suspicion. Search the woods for a body. Go to court. And other stressful situations. So the persisting question is, "What am I supposed to wear?" Casual? Formal? Functional? There are so many things to choose from. Here are a few quick tips and outfits to get you through the next few months.

When you're questioned by the police, you're going to want to look as disheveled as possible. Before you voluntarily go down to the police station the day after your loved one goes missing, you'll want to grab the dirtiest t-shirt you own. You want to look as if you hadn't given any thought to what you were wearing because you're just so worried. Dig through your laundry hamper if you have to. Any sort of food stains will tie this look together. Sweatpants are an absolute must, as you'll be spending several hours in an interrogation room and you'll want to be comfy. Sweatpants are a perfect mix of style and function for these types of situations.

168

When holding a press conference, you'll want to look as pulled together as possible. This will make the community around you feel sympathy and they'll never suspect you. For the men, a crisp blue oxford and light khakis do just the trick. No one wants to help a slob. But avoid ties. You don't want to look too put together. No one wants to help an uppity asshole. For the ladies, a nice, conservative dress gives you a matronly air that people can't help but love and trust. But watch those low necklines. No one wants to help a slut.

When searching the woods for a body, keep your wardrobe functional. Hiking boots are ideal, but if you don't have a pair, some worn-out sneakers will do. Cargo shorts are an absolute must for any search party. You'll want to have those extra pockets to store your flashlight, cellphone, rubber gloves, and a granola bar, in case you get hungry. And don't forget that blood covered hand towel you used to clean up the kitchen. It's the ultimate fashion faux pas to find bloody evidence in your closet so you'll want to find a large body of water and try to get the rags to the bottom. A true fashionista always brings some twine to tie the evidence to a heavy rock before throwing it in the water.

When the police find your loved one wherever you dumped them, the only thing you really need to wear is a look of fear and shock. If your face isn't expressive enough to show sadness, a simple hand over the mouth will do all the work for you. To really pull this look together, scream and fall to the ground. This is a look many won't soon forget.

When you go on trial for homicide, wear your best suit at all times. The jury will think, "Innocent people don't wear suits." If you can, avoid wearing handcuffs. The steel clashes with your tie.

When you go to prison with a life sentence, you don't have to worry about picking out the right outfit.

Unfortunately, everyone looks bad in orange.

Elaine Wood has told stories all her life, many inspired by her home in upper East Tennessee. Her family and friends encouraged her to write her stories down, and the Cohn Creative Writers Workshop inspired her to do so.

Cannonball's Friend

Louis bounced down the rutted, red-clay path that lead the way to Cannonball's house. It was only 7:25 am, but Cannonball had already missed the bus to kindergarten. His dad Bud had caught Louis just in time to hitch ride, "Oh, Dr. Dotson, I hate to ask, but could you please drop Cannonball off at school on your way to Knoxville?" This didn't happen often, so Louis was more than happy to oblige.

Dr. Louis Dotson had been a sociology professor at the University of Tennessee for the better part of his 46 years. He had always believed in giving people a leg up, and that's probably what led him to move into his chosen field.

The little family for whom he had provided a home for the last three years in exchange for random farm work and odd jobs, had moved in and gotten a firm foothold on his heart. There was Bud's sweet, shy nineteen-year old wife, Luella and their

172

three kids, Cannonball, Cassie Cate, and Roy Bennie Buddy, loosely named after his father. There were barely nine months in between each of them.

Cannonball lived at the end of a shady, rock-strewn path. It was hardly wide enough to accommodate Louis's oversized '67 Ford F-100 pick-up with its oversized cab. When he arrived at the modest, whitewashed cinder block house, adjacent to the milking barn, Cannonball was waiting in the freshly mowed front yard, sitting on the side of the rubber tire planter filled with vinca major and red geraniums. He leaped up and came running when he saw the truck pull up.

Louis hopped out, scooped up Cannonball, and hoisted him into the huge cab. His little well-scrubbed face still gave off a sallow glow from the permanent red clay patina on his skin. As they began the long ride back up Hickory Creek Road to the highway, he noticed that Cannonball's little legs weren't even long enough to make the bend at the knee, and the soles of his tiny, well-worn shoes were facing up the path toward Dixie Lee Junction.

Louis felt Cannonball looking at him all the way out to Lee Highway. When he turned his head to face him, Cannonball was already staring him straight in the eyes. As they made eye contact, a big smile of gratitude and affection came over Cannonball's face and he said in the most charming East Tennessee accent, "Hit's nice to have friends, don't it?"

Later that afternoon, when Louis related this experience to his colleagues, he added, "He couldn't have spoken more eloquently had he possessed full command of the King's English!"

The New York Times

https://nyti.ms/2bsET3N

DENMARK

MAYHEM, MADNESS, AND MURDER ROCK ELSINOR CASTLE:

CROWN PRINCE VOWS REVENGE

Prince Hamlet, heir to the throne of Denmark, was called home from university in Wittenberg, Germany last week for the funeral of his father who had died mysteriously eight weeks prior, unbeknownst to the young man. He arrived at the Elsinore Castle and found more shocking news.

His mother Gertrude had already remarried, and the man she married is his Uncle Claudius, the deceased King's brother. Claudius has usurped the throne and declared himself the new King in the middle of all the chaos and disarray.

In a spirited interview with the psychologically distraught, erstwhile heir to the throne, Prince Hamlet exclaimed,

"I smell foul play, and I vow revenge!!"

-whereupon he began to stalk Claudius and the suspicious courtiers around the royal family's manor. In a dramatic and bizarre turn of events, he accidentally, but fatally stabbed Polonius, his girlfriend Ophelia's father, mistaking him for a rat as Polonius eavesdropped behind the curtain to Hamlet confronting his mother.

The castle had been besieged by mayhem and mystery and now, murder. Hamlet was essentially a noble human being of great moral character who had been overtaken by madness and paranoia-truly a great tragedy of Shakespearean proportions.

"I will avenge my father's death!" he screamed.

Hamlet was immobilized by confusion and indecision.

"I want to find my father's murderer, but it's not an issue of impropriety or ill- gotten gains," he said. "I am still trying to decide whether I want to be or not to be king; that is the question."

It is feared that Ophelia has also been the victim of foul play, but reports were still unconfirmed at press time.

Scott Wiley is a freelance curriculum writer and editor. He enjoys writing all kinds of fiction and poetry. Originally from Texas, Scott and his wife now live in Hermitage, Tennessee.

Clutter

Unresolved projects and old bank
statements. Islands grow into continents
Narrowing the navigable spaces of my
office.

Boxed-up dreams and fragmented ideas.
Old issues stacked up like magazines.
Worries, fears, and lingering nightmares.
Crowding the corners of mind and memory.
Memory and mind.

Hoarding and holding on.
Packing away and piling up.
Defying the calm and peaceful soul,
I seek to be.

A Simple Way to Build Good Readers

Reading requires lots of skills—identifying letters, understanding the sounds they make, blending those sounds into words, building language. When we think about teaching young children to read, often we think about activities and drills that will help children recognize letters and repeat sounds for those letters. Developing good readers begins before a child even knows what a letter is.

Jim Trelease, educator and author of *The Read Aloud Handbook*, stresses that reading books to children is a foundational way to build pre-literacy skills. "Pre-literacy" signifies the skills necessary for a child to be ready to learn to read. One way to build these skills is by reading aloud, which builds a child's vocabulary.

"The one prekindergarten skill that matters above all others because it is the prime predictor of school success or failure is the child's vocabulary entering school," Trelease says.

While reading aloud helps all kids gain vocabulary, it can especially aid kids from lower socio-economic homes. In a study conducted by Hart and Risley, preschoolers from families on welfare had significantly smaller vocabularies than children of the same age in professional families, up to fifty percent less vocabulary size.

They found that the words of a child's vocabulary are directly related to the words in a parent's vocabulary. Follow up studies by Hart and Risley found that these gaps held true for these children when they reached third grade-- the children with more limited vocabularies at an earlier age tested lower on language and reading comprehension skills.

Reading skills begin at an early age when the child is not even aware of print. Reading books to young children can build vocabulary by providing new words in context. Printed materials contain "rarer" words that go beyond everyday conversation and make up a large part of educational language. For example, a child who hears stories with descriptive language will begin to understand different ways to describe things. Books will use a variety of words to refer to objects in the world. Hearing books read can help a child build a bank of words, even if those words are not used by his parents.

Although hearing words used in different contexts like books or in conversation is helpful, it is not enough. Children must begin to speak and use them in their own conversations. Adults can encourage this by talking with the child about books after reading.

Reading and literacy are hot topics in our society. Education reform dominates the elections and legislation of many cities and states and even on the national level. One way to build literacy skills is to offer intervention to more disadvantaged students and reading to children. It seems so simple--and maybe that's why it's overlooked. What child could hear a book read by you today?

Friends in Lines of Gray

The need for words, an escape,
pulls me in.

Adventures on a distant planet,
murders and investigations,
the regular life of someone else.

The need is greedy.
I lose myself among the lines of gray.

Invisible, outside the gray,
my true friends are hobbits
and Belgian detectives and
teenagers lost in a dystopian land.

The ones I seek
live among pages and between dusty
jackets.
I know each time they will greet me,
welcome me with open arms.
There is no rejection.

Literary friends may stay ever true
yet their arms do little to warm me through.

Losing the Curse

Jim lay face down on the bed, pretending to sleep. He heard Lucinda moving about the room. A drawer slid open and he heard her rummage through it for a couple minutes. He felt the bed sink as she sat on the side of it. From the movement, he assumed she was putting on socks and shoes. The legs of her jeans swished as she moved to tie each shoe.

She shifted again and Jim smelled her shampoo as she leaned over him. Her lips brushed his cheek. "See you later," she whispered. Jim heard steps retreat. The front door opened and closed. The lock snapped into place. She was gone.

Jim lay there a few more minutes, debating whether to get up or not. He had nowhere to be, no one expecting him. No job for over a year.

"You must be cursed or something," his sister told him just last week. "I hear about

a teacher shortage and you can't get a job."
Jim huffed as he thought about Sarah. *She's
so encouraging. Always had been like that.*

He closed his eyes, expelling his sister and
picturing Lucinda. The long strands of brown
hair that hung like Spanish moss on either
side of her thin, pale face. The dark brown
eyes, almost black, piercing you with a
discerning gaze. A mouth, quick with
encouraging comment or quick with a laugh
that such a woman stayed with him, he
couldn't guess. *Maybe she's the one's that
cursed*, Jim thought.

Jim sat up and shook away the thought
crawling through his brain. He looked
around; the room certainly reinforced the
idea of a curse. The carpet was comfortable
under foot but spotted with stains of
indeterminate origin. Outdated furniture
looking well worn. A dusty, musty smell.
Why was Lucinda still here?

Maybe today would be the day things would
change. Maybe the curse breaker was just
waiting for him around the corner. He stood
and moved to the bathroom, then shaved

the graying stubble from his cheeks and chin. A small handful of gel helped set his hair into an agreeable arrangement that hid the thinning spots and silver strands.

He pulled on his best blue shirt and dark pants. Carefully, deliberately, he knotted a yellow tie and appraised the look in the mirror. Deciding that he needed just a little more, he pulled a gray sweater vest over his head to complete the look.

He sat at the scarred and littered desk, tapping on his computer for a half hour. The printer spit out his compiled list of private schools. "Better in person than email or phone," he said to his reflection as he checked one more time to make sure the image was right. He grabbed the portfolio of resumes and strode out the front door, confident and ready.

Two hours and five schools later, that confidence had ebbed away. He sat in the outer office of Preston Prep. The room had an air of casual busyness, anticipation of something coming, knowing that the onslaught was still a few weeks away.

People wandered in and out intermittently. They spoke to a small woman dressed in a pale green top and matching skirt. Her hair was pulled back in a severe twist that looked several decades too old for her. She wore a bracelet with small bells, charms on one wrist. The office was her domain.

She dispatched each person with a short answer and no small talk. She repeatedly collated groups of papers and slid them into manila folders. She scooped the forms with machine-like precision. Form, form, form, form, form, form, handbook, and form. Into the envelope, over and over, the bracelet on her wrist jingled an accompaniment to her work.

Jim sat and waited and waited and watched. At first the jingle of the bracelet and the efficient work of the secretary were enjoyable, almost calming. But after a while, the sound began to wear on him. He watched the sweep of the second hand on the clock move above the secretary's head. The phone rang a few times. Each caller received a pleasant greeting, a brief answer, and a quick good-bye.

When the second hand had made the clock's circuit over six hundred times, Jim stood. The secretary stopped in mid-collate and looked up at him.

"I know that Mr. Hinson is busy and I had no appointment," Jim said. He swallowed and cleared his throat, hoping the secretary didn't think he sounded as whiny and desperate as he sounded to himself. "I can come back later if that would be better, but I would really like to talk with him."

The secretary stared hard. Then Jim saw her soften, just slightly. "Let me check and see if he will be much longer," she said.

She finished the stack she was assembling and stuffed it into an envelope. She stood and moved through a door in the back of the room, the jingling bracelet accenting her steps.

Jim wandered over to the display on the wall. Pictures of sports teams and band rehearsals. Younger kids dressed in animal costumes. Families on blankets spread on the ground, eating sandwiches and snow cones. Amid the photos were a few certificates. Preston Prep had donated to the local food bank and received academic recognition at a regional competition. Jim read through all the commendations and appreciations.

He walked back to his chair but didn't sit, watching the second-hand sweep around the clock another time or two. He heard the faint jingle that announced the secretary's return.

"Mr. Hinson can see you now," she said.

Jim pushed through a small swinging door that separated the visitor area from the rest of the office. He followed the jingling secretary through the door in the back and down a narrow hallway. She stopped and indicated the office at the end of the hall. Jim passed her and paused at the office doorway.

A man in his twenties sat behind a narrow desk. Every square inch of the desk was covered with folders, papers, and books. Shelves behind the man held a variety of books, a basketball, some hats, a ship in a bottle, and a stuffed iguana. A laptop rested on the windowsill.

The man stood. He was shorter than Jim with blonde hair and a thin strip of a beard around the jawline. He moved around the desk, extended a hand, and smiled.

"Stanton Hinson," he said as they shook hands.

"Jim Case. I appreciate your time, Mr. Hinson."

Hinson waved off the comment and moved to a small card table in the corner of the office. "Let's sit over here," he said.

Jim handed a resume to Hinson and perched on a metal chair. Hinson skimmed through the text and set it aside.

"Mr. Case," Hinson said, "as far as I'm aware, all of our staff are returning. We have no openings for teachers."

Jim swallowed the growing lump in his throat. "What about the educational assistant position you listed on Ed-Jobs?"

"Well," Hinson said, "we have not filled that position yet. That is a contingent position. We will not fill it unless our enrollment requires it." Hinson paused. "Besides, that position is an hourly, level one position. It doesn't require a licensed teacher or even a college degree. You are very over-qualified."

"Does that mean I wouldn't be considered?"

Hinson smiled slightly. "Compensation for that position would not match your level of education or experience, and as I said, that position is contingent. We would not even fill that position until after enrollment has been secured."

"I see." Jim looked at this man, half his age, who was deciding his fate. Jim wanted to punch him right on that strip of beard. But it wasn't Hinson's fault that Jim was over-qualified and over-age and overdue for a break.

Jim stood suddenly. Hinson was on his feet in an instant.

"Thank you again for your time, I know you have many other things to do." Jim moved across the office and to the hall.

"Mr. Case?" Hinson followed. "May I keep your resume? I almost always get a last summer surprise, a teacher whose plans change at the last minute. Something could open up."

"Yes. Thank you, Mr. Hinson. You've been most kind."

They walked together through the front office to the small swinging door.

Hinson touched Jim's shoulder. "Mr. Case, if we need that educational assistant, I'll call you. Just to check if you're still in the market." Hinson shook Jim's hand again. "Good luck, Mr. Case."

193

Jim sat the car outside Preston Prep. He looked at his list of schools. Still a few possibilities on the list, and plenty of resumes in the portfolio. Jim sighed. Still other days to face those rejections. Wait another day to fight that curse. He headed home.

He changed into a t-shirt and jeans. He looked around the old place. Still ways to be productive.

Jim hauled the vacuum cleaner from the closet. He ran it over every inch of the stained comfortable carpet. He washed the dishes from dinner last night. He scoured the kitchen sink and all the bathroom fixtures. He even dusted the tables and aligned the books on the shelves.

He glanced at the old rooster clock in the kitchen. Almost time for Lucinda. He'd surprise her. He checked the refrigerator and the pantry to see what was available. "It's comfort food tonight," he decided.

Jim set the large skillet on the stove and added some oil. He chopped an onion and dropped the pieces in the oil with a satisfying sizzle. He adjusted the temperature so the onions would cook and not burn.

While they released a pleasing aroma into the air, he peeled some potatoes and cut them into small chunks. He stirred the onions and added the potatoes. He pulled open the can of Spam and slid the block of meat from the can.

After running the meat under water and dabbing it dry, he carefully cut it into cubes. He dropped the meat into the pan and stirred to mix the potatoes and Spam. After a couple of minutes, he reduced the temperature again and covered the pan with a lid.

He hummed to himself as he put away the dried dishes. He set the table and stirred the food in the pan, putting the lid back on. He looked around the room, making sure everything was just as he wanted it.

In that moment, Jim knew his sister was wrong. He had no curse; he was a blessed man. They had a place to live and made enough to keep it. They would get by until something else came. And he had Lucinda. Yes, he was a blessed man.

He smiled as he heard the front door open. Lucinda was home.

A New Day

Claire carefully centered the chair on the bay window. She dropped into the soft cushions and stared at the window as if it were a television. The sky moved from black to gray to pinkish yellow. She watched the changing show, absently tracing the lines of the nearby carved wooden box.

"He's not coming back." Her words echoed in the sitting room, underlining the emptiness of the house. She wasn't sure why she spoke aloud. She could have just as easily thought it. But the spoken words reassured her and terrified her. Somehow the sounds made the situation a reality and not just a stray nightmare from last night.

The changing colors of the sky reminded her of a painting she saw years ago. An Edward Hopper, full of realism in the pink skies. She had a small postcard print of it somewhere. A small rectangle of peacefulness. How she wished she could hold peacefulness in her hand as she had that card.

She had seen the painting and bought the card on one of their trips together. A beach town not far away from this one. She hated the beach, sand nestled everywhere that followed her back into whatever house or rooms she stayed. The bright beach sun cooked her skin, reddening every sliver that peeked from sleeve edges or hem lines. And she would happily never look at another seagull in flight or sun glint on the ocean surface.

The sun was brighter now. Claire continued to trace the lines of the box, a slight smile as she thought about him. He was born for the beach.

Each holiday, he strode along the shore with a bare chest and brief swimsuit. His skin darkened to a nice cappuccino. She did enjoy running her fingers along the lines in his chest, among the dark hairs that grew there. Down his stomach to the swimsuit edge.

198

On the good days, he smiled at her and ran a finger gently along her jaw line. As she watched, he swam out and back in strong strokes. Then he'd join her under the umbrella, and they talked as they traced one another. A gentle kiss reminded her of all the reasons she married him. They'd walk together, leading the sand into their room. On these good days, she ignored the sand and focused on him.

But lately the bad days had outnumbered the good ones. Practically swallowed all the possible good ones whole. On those days, he flinched if she touched him, barked if she spoke. If he touched her, it was to push her hand away. Sometimes he shoved more than just her hand.

On those days, she walked back alone to their rooms. She'd shower to rid herself as much as possible of the dreaded sand, then find a quiet corner to read herself to sleep. He would be elsewhere. Hours or even days later, he appeared to collapse in the bed.

199

Claire blinked away the memories. He would not be back this time. Whatever days were coming ahead, he would not be in them.

Claire pushed herself out of the chair. The day was fully lit now. "I'm not coming back," she said. She spoke to the carved box, to the sun past the window, to herself and the world.

She walked to the hall and picked up her small bag. She looked back into the sitting room, the chair, the box, and the window. She nodded, lifted her chin, and walked out the front door. Someone else could spread his ashes or mind the intricate box that held him. She had places to go and none of them would have a beach.

Resolution

The new year here
  Time to list
The ways I can be better

Drop the pounds
  Walk the walk
Become a real go-getter

The list is made
  The plans are strong
I'm ready to begin

But two weeks pass
  In this new year
And I'm myself again

201

Progressive Stories

The 1960's: Up Close and Personal

James Currey, Louan Tillman, & Julie Kramer

The 1960's were a tumultuous time in the United States. The culture of the 1950's ran headlong into a new generation that saw the world with different eyes. We saw our leaders assassinated, an inexplicable war break out, brand new music styles born of chaos and confusion. We watched with wonder as our fellow citizens explored another world.

There seemed to be a generational clash in how people defined what it meant to be a citizen of America. The Civil Rights Movement peaked during the 1960's; the norm at the start of the decade was that the races were to be completely segregated. Nationally and locally, we wrestled with the issues of the changing times and the upheaval in the world as we knew it.

Following are the reflections, impressions, and creative interpretations of three ordinary citizens who lived through some of the most challenging and divisive times yet to face our country. Julie, a 58 year old, spent the 1960's in Memphis, Atlanta, and Nashville. Louan was born and grew up in Nashville. Jim, 68, was born in Nashville, but spent time in Cookeville, Washington DC, and Memphis and is retired from the US Air Force.

Assassination of the President

Louan

I had to know. I couldn't explain my need then and I still can't now but I had to know. The how, the what, the who and the why- I had to know. Why those kids no longer had a daddy and she no longer had a mate. Why that big, pretty family lost a brother and a son on that awful day in Dallas. I was only six, but I knew it mattered--mattered to us all. I don't recall even knowing what a president was but I somehow knew that this man mattered.

So I read and I studied. Everything I could find-- all the papers, reports, and books written that might offer insight. Conspiracy theories, multiple gunmen, the Cubans, the Mafia, the FBI and the CIA. I studied them all. Second by second of that horrible yet riveting film. As I got older Dallas became a pilgrimage with Dealey Plaza holy ground. The sixth floor of that dusty book building a shrine to something I could not and still do not understand.

I should never have had a reason to even think the words Mannlicher-Carcano much less know of the devastation one could cause in the hands of a man living a life gone horribly wrong. And yet I do, just as I know how long it takes to get to Parkland Hospital when the roads are cleared ahead of you. And bullet trajectories that make no sense but are true nonetheless. I know because I had to know--to try to make sense of something that didn't and still doesn't. My first encounter with senseless violence left a lasting impression because no matter how much I know I will never understand.

Jim

It was a day like most days for a high school freshman. Our football season was just over and the rigors of athletic competition melted away into a whimsical state of relaxation. It was time to apply myself to the rigors of academia.

My morning was filled with homeroom activities and preparation for the coming onslaught of science, math, English and history. Drinking from the firehose of knowledge excited me. My usual world was small, self-contained, and comfortable. Nothing much existed outside the confines of Nashville and the local small-town atmosphere and country music culture. But to learn about other worlds. That was something.

Around noon as students gathered in the cafeteria for our daily dose of institutional nourishment. It wasn't great, though it was comfortable and filled a familiar place in my life. There was the usual nonsense that occurs when you place adolescents near food. Most of it was consumed. Some of it became projectiles to annoy certain people and the rest became the food of choice for animals who occupied a lower space on the food chain. Nature in action and reaction.

Then it began. That low murmur of many conversations beginning like a string of fireworks. He was dead. Who was dead? The voices and sounds of disbelief flowed through the crowd as smoke on the wind. It became louder and people began to gasp and cry. Who was dead? The question echoed and bounced off the walls.

The president was dead. Which president? Our president? Do you mean, our country's president? Yes. The news took me by utter surprise. How can this be? It can't be. No. I know very little about what was going on in the world outside Nashville, but in one blinding flash of knowledge I became a citizen of the world.

Our leader had fallen prey to the evil hand of an assassin. Our President, John F. Kennedy was gone in the blink of an eye. Who was to lead us? How would we survive as a nation? Suddenly I felt small and helpless to the undercurrents that swirl around us. How would I survive. If someone could kill a President, anyone could be killed.

The crowd in the cafeteria slowly disbursed to take up their studies, but the air about us had changed, and our lungs, our minds, could notice the difference. It happened like most monumental events. Life slowly traverses the cavern between birth and death in a seemingly constant ribbon. Each day seems to be a carbon copy of the last. You come to expect very few changes from one rising to the next. Then the incredible happens. The journey takes an incalculable diversion. That was the way it was November 11th, 1963. The day Kennedy died.

Julie

Lizzie sat in the vinyl-covered chair in the den crying. During all the time we spent together, I never saw Lizzie cry, although she had wiped my tears plenty of times. She was a great comforter and she was a momma to all the little kids in my family even though she wasn't our blood momma. She was that perfect combination of sugar and spice. She loved me tenderly and disciplined me strictly.

I climbed into Lizzie's lap and nestled against her neck. She always smelled good, like she had just gotten out of the tub. Her wiry hair was in a tousled bun and the loose strands tickled my face. I pulled myself closer to her and could feel the buttons of her white uniform dress. Reactively, she put her arms around me. The closer I got, the louder she sobbed. "Lizzie, are you sick?" I asked.

"Child, the president has been killed."

"Was he sick?" I asked.

Moon Landing

Louan

"Can you believe it?" Yuri asked Valentina. "We will plant the hammer and sickle at least a year before those crazy Americans even get off the ground. All their people will think their claims are a hoax or some big Hollywood movie."

That is how I imagine the dialogue went when the cosmonauts sat around tossing back fermented potato juice, and they had every reason to be cocky. The Soviets launched Laika, the dog in 1957 and Yuri Gagarin in 1961, so it seemed almost inevitable that they would get to the moon first. Using early German technology and German scientists bolstered by the work of Soviet Sergei Korolev, they had the first spacewalk, the first lunar impact, the first soft unmanned landing, the first photos of the dark side and the first lunar rover. They even had the first woman in space, Valentina Tereshkova. So why then did their space program suddenly crash and burn-- literally?

I'm sure there are hundreds of reasons, explanations, and excuses. Did the U.S. sabotage it as has been speculated? Was it the untimely deaths of key figures Korolev and Gagarin? Maybe it was the introduction of the newer, heavier N1 propulsion system that never made it off the launch pad that caused the program to fail. I suspect a combination of all of that and the challenge laid down by a charismatic upstart of a U.S. President who truly believed that we could do anything.

"Find a way," he told our people. "Make it happen." But did we *need* to go to the moon?

It is not for me to say. I know that many technological advances came from the space program and that is a good thing. But the idea was to beat the Russians there. The national pride we felt when we made it happen was something you never forget even if the young president did not live to see it happen. The spirit that we can do anything lives on even today in the poster that hangs in my office that says, "Don't tell me the sky's limit when there are footprints on the moon."

We believed it then. We believe it now. And I believe that beating the Soviets to the moon goes a long way toward explaining the unshakeable sense that there is no challenge that we cannot overcome.

Jim

It was the evening of July 20th, 1969. Sitting in the home of my mother and father in law, I joined millions of people around the world in watching a live television report from NASA.

The Soviet Union had taken the first step into outer space by launching the Sputnik earth satellite in 1957. Our civilization had never done anything like this before. We were earth-bound creatures who gazed at the heavens but realized we lacked the ingenuity and capability to reach beyond the layer of atmosphere we knew to be home.

At the time of Sputnik, I was learning basic mathematics and building sentences in third grade. Yet, even then I felt the romance of space travel. Oceans had been crossed and air space navigated by pioneers of exploration. Yet, we were confined to our limited space in the universe. Outer space was the new frontier. From that time on, my life was filled with the dream of becoming part of this bright new human adventure.

My education took a definitive path. I knew technology was the way to outer space, so my coursework was filled with classes in math and science. If I was to be part of the team, I had to speak the language.

As I followed news of the space race, the Soviet Union was headway, launching more satellites and even a manned spacecraft. We were lagging in technology and exploration, but there was a bright light just ahead. In 1961, our President John F. Kennedy announced the United States was setting a goal of putting a man on the moon by the end of the decade.

Fast forward to 1969. I was an undergraduate at Tennessee Tech University studying mechanical engineering. I knew what was needed to escape the earth's gravitational field and travel the 240,000 miles to the moon. That was the equivalent of thirty times the diameter of the earth. Everything had to work flawlessly. One small error and our astronautics would be lost in space forever.

That evening in 1969 was filled with excitement and wonder. Would we do it? I watched as the moon was circumnavigated by Apollo 11. The lunar lander reached the surface and one, then two men walked on our moon. We did it. Our civilization was never to be the same. We surpassed our bounds and traveled through a desolate environment to occupy another heavenly body.

Julie

When I looked into the sky, the moon and the stars seemed make-believe. How could it be that someone could fly there, to what seemed imaginary? How would you even know which way to turn to get there? Nobody had ever been there or touched anything to prove that it was even real. The live feed seemed grainy, but nonetheless, it was clear that history was being made that day. The first man on the moon had landed and I was watching history unfold with my family on our console T.V.

It seemed so strange to think men were on the moon and I was watching this live in my den. I don't believe I had ever seen anything on live T.V. before. I was scared the astronauts might float away and be in limbo forever. As a child, I couldn't fully understand the science of it all. The landing seemed more magical than scientific. "One small step for man, one giant leap for mankind," Neil Armstrong said. I didn't fully understand that profound statement then.

The year was 1969 and the moon landing proved that we Americans were the winners of the race. For me, 1969 also signified the year my family moved to Nashville so my father could open a store at Nashville's first mall, 100 Oaks. It was also the year I received my first kiss from Kerry Dye in a friend's backyard. As a young girl, my life was centered around myself and the people within immediate reach. Seeing Neil Armstrong walk on the moon struck a chord with me. There's a whole universe out there, and I am just one tiny speck in it.

Vietnam War

Louan

I wasn't even born when this war started back in the 1950's, but I remember growing up with the escalation through the 1960's and the terrible split it caused not just in our country but in my own home. My grandfather was a Navy man, so most of my family was very supportive of the military in this war. My older brother intended to enlist as soon as he was old enough, but for the life of me, I could not understand why we needed to be in that faraway place defending our national interests. What was the point? Granted I was very young, but it never made sense.

I watched the news every night as the battles raged and names like Gen, Westmoreland, the Tet Offensive, and Saigon became commonplace around our dinner table. The news that President Johnson would not seek re-election was widely discussed as well. Everybody knew it had to do with his escalation of the war and the way he misled the American public. We all knew young men who were already being shipped off in spite of the "don't tell anybody" rules the military had in place about where they were going.

The war became very personal for me when one of my classmates came to school and told us her older brother Ronnie had been killed in Vietnam. Then came the news stories of the atrocities of My Lai and the Green Beret affair and a story that then president Nixon had sent armed nuclear missiles to the border of the Soviet Union in an effort to get us (and them) out of the war.

It seemed that the entire world had gone mad. Protesters were everywhere. Even returning soldiers were protesting that we had no business there. My parents changed their tune and supported my brother when he postponed his enlistment plan and started college instead. I remember the very clear shift in our house and in my friends. We began wearing tie-dye, Nehru jackets, love beads, and peace signs. Conversations were less about the war and more about the protests. Tumultuous times for our family and our country.

Jim

Vietnam first entered my life by way of rumor in 1965. At the time, I was a sixteen-year-old high school sophomore. Vietnam was a strange and mysterious place somewhere in Southeast Asia. Former high school football teammates from 1963 and 1964 were swept up into the U.S. Army after graduation. The rumors told of some who had been killed in Vietnam. I was thrust into an immediate state of awareness. Would this be my fate? I needed to know more.

As I understood it, the United States was assisting the Government of South Vietnam to defend themselves   against Communist guerillas from North Vietnam. Following World War Two, the French had tried to manage Vietnam only to have been cast out of the country, which divided itself into a Chinese Communist-aligned portion and a Western-aligned portion. The Communists

218

in the north were eager to absorb their southern neighbors. This was a threat to the democratic stability of the entire region and thus became a focus of our foreign policy. In the early 1960's, we tried military assistance which later turned to military support. At one time, the United States had over half a million troops deployed in support of the Vietnam War.

So, how did this affect me? I began watching the television news and reading newspaper accounts of the conflict. It seemed that Americans were dying every day. It wasn't long until our thirst for military personnel exceeded our supply. Our government turned to conscription. All men aged eighteen and older were to register for the draft. That meant I could be drafted into the military and would probably be sent to Vietnam.

This triggered my instinct for proactivity. I knew that I loved my country, and if she was threatened, I needed to respond. I could graduate from high school and accept my fate or I could make the best of a bad situation. College was in my sights and I knew there was a way to satisfy all my needs. If I was going into the military, I wanted to go as an officer. I remained in college long enough to receive an engineering degree and participate in the university Reserve Officer Training Corps. Along with my degree in engineering, I was also commissioned a Second Lieutenant in the US Army.

As fate would have it, the Vietnam War ended about the time I graduated from college. I received military training and turned out to be in the civilian population. This situation presented me with another opportunity. Not only could I be a civil engineer, but I could continue a military career. Eventually, my military career spanned more than thirty years.

What impact did Vietnam have on me? It allowed me to give to my country and experience things I would not have otherwise been able to do. It was a pivotal point in this country's history and I was in the position to witness it firsthand.

Music

Louan

I remember a friend, a much older friend, had a monster crush on the Beatles. All of the Beatles. It was all she ever wanted to talk about. That was my first exposure to music of the '60's. I must have listened to those early Beatles tunes a million times. Then she moved away and suddenly I had no more Beatles since she owned all the records, but the times they were a changing anyway.

The increasing opposition to the Vietnam War spawned a new kind of music. The protest songs were much more to my liking as I preferred the folksy singer songwriter style with deep and meaningful lyrics. People like Bob Dylan, Joan Baez, Pete Seeger, and Nina Simone captured the anger felt by the nation at having their sons shipped off to a foreign land only to come home in body bags. Anger at how the war was being fought only by the lower classes since the "Fortunate Sons" were allowed a pass on the "mandatory" conscription.

Then the soldiers started coming home after their tours and we had the rise of the drug culture songs. So many came home with drug habits and a new appreciation for mindless head bobbing songs that last for hours that an entirely new subculture was born. "Get high music" we called it. People listened to the same thing over, over and over again for hours. LSD use was so rampant that some songs even celebrated it--White Rabbit by Jefferson Airplane is one that comes to mind that was popular at my school.

I don't think there is any doubt that the music of the 1960's was a mirror of the tumultuous times. In hindsight, the early days of the suit-wearing Beatles seem so tame compared to the late 60's hippie fest known as Woodstock where there was a real "anything goes" attitude that carried over into the early 1970's. Innocence, protest, rebellion, sex, drugs and rock and roll. The music of the '60's had it all.

Jim

The decade of the 60's began with the Beach Boys and ended with Woodstock. In between were two distinctive eras of music that reflected the turmoil and creativity of our culture. As an eleven-year-old in sixth grade, I listened to the sounds of the Greatest Generation and classical music. This was a familiar genre for me because it served as background music for cartoons. Strange as it seems now, Baby Boomers grew up on classical music presented with animated skits that taught moral lessons.

The dividing line came in 1963 when the British Invasion occurred. Music from the Beatles burst upon the scene as I entered 9th grade. Time was ripe for experimentation and the hard beat of the Byrd's, the Rolling Stones and the Buckingham's. It was a time for protest over the emerging war in Vietnam, racial tensions and political disconnectedness. Baby Boomers were making a statement of their culture. They had enough of the world and swore to change it.

I entered college in 1967 to study engineering and took music with me. It was the preferred language of expression and connected people from distant corners of the world. As our music became angrier, the war escalated and the deaths of Martin Luther King and Robert Kennedy in 1968 gave rise to civil unrest.

The decade came to an end, and so did Janis Joplin, Jimi Hendrix, and Brian Jones, all from drug overdoses. The world was changing and our music expressed our similarly fluctuating emotions. The music of the 60's was full of stories that live on today every time we play those old records.

Julie

The first album I ever owned was the Monkees debut album. It was released in 1967. I was seven and Mickey was my favorite Monkee. In my world in Nashville, Tennessee, I went to school with children of some of the great country singers of that time: Ernest Tubb, Mel Tillis, and Jerry Reed. My step-father played in some of the great combo bands of that time: The

Chessman, The Counts, and Key Largo. These combos played at VFW Halls, Moose Lodges, weddings, and any other special occasion they could book.   That was my little world of music.

But the world was a big place and the 1960's may have been the greatest era of music ever. The list of popular singers, groups, and songwriters includes the biggest names of all times.

The 60's introduced the British invasion and the biggest group of that time was the Beatles. Their first number one hit "I Want to Hold Your Hand" hit the top of the charts in 1964. The 60's also produced the Rolling Stones, Led Zeppelin, Fleetwood Mac, Eric Clapton, Pink Floyd, The Who, Jimi Hendrix, and The Doors. Elvis Presley was at the height of his career in the 1960's. The turbulence of the Civil Rights Movement and the Vietnam War produced music written to make a statement. Joan Baez, Bob Dylan, and Joni Mitchell were some of the leaders in that movement.

Motown gave birth to the Supremes, the Temptations, the Four Tops, and Marvin Gaye. Rounding out the 60's was the Jackson Five. The music of the 60's continues to be some of the most popular music of today and is enjoyed just as much as it was fifty years ago.

Conclusion

We all were witness to the 1960's, it was a time of turmoil and change, but also a time of emergence and creativity. We've touched on just a few of the primary events of the decade: American entered a war in Southeast Asia, we ushered in the Civil Rights Act, and placed a human on the moon. It was also a time of great tragedy as we lost three of the finest among us: Dr. Martin Luther King, Robert Kennedy, and John F. Kennedy. These events mean different things to each of us because of our age, background, culture and perspective. These memories are a part of us, as your experiences are and will be a part of you.

Murder on Rabbit Trap Road

Holly Achurch, Tom Jamison, &
Denise Sheehan

It was a cool October night, and Officer Nick
Moyers wanted to be carving pumpkins
instead of standing at the barricade. Every
year on the weekend before Halloween,
Colts Creek held its Autumn Bash.
Downtown was closed to cars and kids took
their costumes for a test run, asking for
candy at the shops lining Clover Street.
Three patrol cars were more than necessary
for one closed block, but having the officers
out with the community helped build
relationships, or so the sergeant said.

All of the cars' radios buzzed around 9pm,
and Nick opened his patrol car door, ready
to assure the dispatcher, Simon, that the
Bash was going smoothly. A hit-and-run
came through the line instead. Reported
over on Rabbit Trap Road, a car had
smashed into the side of the reporting
driver and fled the scene. A DUI, most
likely. It didn't happen often in Colts Creek,

but when it did, it was always the same people.

Nick took the call, since he was the first on the phone, and told the other two officers that he had to go. Kalowski assured him that they had things under control down here, among the ghosts and the superheroes. She was always quick with sarcasm, which Nick appreciated.

The patrol car drove slowly, with an even slower rotation of the lights. Didn't see the need to blast the siren too. He waved to the people he didn't recognize, and said goodnight to the people he did. It was a twenty-minute drive to where he was headed. 103.9 FM was organizing the Bash and they were playing Halloween songs all weekend. "Thriller" was on, for the fourth time today.

"You hear the door slam and realize there's nowhere left to run
You feel the cold hand and wonder if you'll ever see the sun

*You close your eyes and hope that
this is just imagination*
Girl but all the while
*You hear a creature creeping up
behind*
You're outta time"

Moyers arrived at 9:40 p.m., taking his time to enjoy the October air. He talked with the Simon the way over. No injuries, no rush, and the driver hit had AAA on the way. Nick didn't know Stephanie Wilson, the driver, but according to Simon she was calm, just a bit shaken up. That stretch of Rabbit Trap was dark, with street lights spread way further than you needed them, sprawling estates leaving acres of wood between driveways.

He was told that the accident was by the Vommer house, which was a nice surprise. The author didn't usually get much traffic, and Nick was hoping he'd get the chance to swing by, ask Ralph Vommer if he'd saw anything, get a "No," and have a chance at small talk with a Pulitzer winner.

When Nick pulled up, Stephanie frantically waved him down. She was already hard to miss, high beams and hazards on in the middle of the road. She was upset that he had taken so long. He explained that things were a bit tied up with the Bash.

"Are you telling me the entire departments at the Bash?" she asked.
The truth was yes, but Nick told her there was another patrol car tied up on the other side of town. Nick asked her to tell him what happened.

"Well, I was coming back from the festival around 8:30. I live about a mile down Rabbit Trap. I was almost there when a car came speeding out of the driveway. It didn't have any headlights on at all! I think it must have been a drunk person, driving like that in the night like this.

Hit me right in the front! If it were any closer, they would've gone straight into my door. I can't believe the airbags didn't go off... I can't believe someone would get behind the wheel like that..." She stopped and sighed.

Nick asked her if she knew when AAA was supposed to arrive. She had just spoken to the driver before Nick pulled up; the tow truck was about ten minutes out. Nick asked her if it was alright if he headed up to the Vommer house and ask about who had just left. He could probably get more information from Vommer himself and radio back in to everyone back at the Bash. Wouldn't be hard to spot a wrecked-up car, and with most of the town already out, a dangerous driver was the last thing the department needed. Nick left the patrol car lights cycling and told Stephanie he would be right back.

The sides of the driveway were lined with lamps, but the ones on the end had been run over, broken glass interspersed in the wood chips. Nick imagined Vommer would be cooperative, especially if the driver had done so much damage.

The author mostly kept to himself, at the end of a long, winding driveway. Nick had never actually seen the house before, but Nick had met Vommer before out in the town. He was a good guy, an honorary librarian who would drop-by the Children's section and hold impromptu story times.

He spoke at the middle school every year right before summer vacation, urging the kids to spend their free time productively with a book. He always passed out bookmarks that read: "Reading is a passport to a world of adventure!" Nick had read one of Vommer's books once, about a rural man who moved to a big city on a whim to start a brand-new life. Vommer wrote all about the interesting shops that lined the streets, the neighborhoods of cultures he didn't know existed, the heart of the city, a massive river directly in the center of downtown. Nick got curious and googled how far away the place was. Turned out, it didn't exist.

There was only one car in the driveway when Nick reached the front of the house. A newer red Chrysler, license plate RU857T. It looked like the side of the car had gotten a bit dented on the rear bumper, with a paint scratch that matched the damage on Stephanie's car. Nick didn't know what kind of car Vommer drove, but wrote it down to check, once he got back to the car.

The house was massive, a venerable mansion, with a porch wrapped all the way around, and a backyard that went off into the darkness of woods. But there were plenty of lights on in the house. Vommer was home.

Nick walked up the front steps and saw the front door was ajar. He rang the doorbell and listened to its chime through the crack of the door. No response. He waited a moment, rung again, and yelled, "Police, anybody home?" He knocked on the door as loudly as he could and pushed the door open slightly. A broken vase lay in the middle of the foyer, flowers wilted in a pool of water, a trail of blood leading further into the house. He called out again into the house to no response, and against his better judgement, stepped through the door.

The room to his left was filled with cardboard boxes without markings, and the room to the right was shut, a double door. Nick followed the blood deeper into the house. The trail was long, going all the way through the winding hallway that seemed to double back on itself. At the end, Nick found another open door. As Nick approached the room, he yelled "Police! Identify yourself!"

Instead of silence, Nick heard the crackle of a fire. Nick walked into a wood paneled study with bookshelves toppled and chairs overturned. Hundreds of individual pages were set aflame in the study's fireplace. On the ground was a body, face down in a pool of blood. Pulitzer Prize winning author, Colts Creek resident, and honorary librarian Ralph Vommer was dead.

Nick knelt down to feel for a pulse. It was his first time in a room with a dead body, or even seeing a dead body. He hoped he was alone. The lights on throughout the house and the closed doors to the front room gave him pause. He regretted that his only radio was back in the patrol car. Rather than wait to report, he looked around the study for a land line and made his way to it—carefully avoiding stepping in the blood, all of his senses on full alert. With so little crime in Colt's Creek, officers rarely carried weapons, especially not on the night of the Autumn Bash.

When he reached Simon, he immediately cut through the usual banter and asked to speak to the sergeant. After an eternity, he relayed the basics to Sergeant McKeon and asked him to send all available backup, including a crime scene unit and a coroner, knowing full well that they would likely come from Lumbertown, the closest town with a full-on police force. He assumed the highway patrol might be of some help, certainly in looking for the alleged getaway car. McKeon cursed, asked a more few questions, then told him to move his patrol car to secure the scene. Hopefully the wrecker service had taken Stephanie Wilson and her car away. She would still need to be interviewed again to get any details about the car, but she didn't need to know all this now. She was lucky that a quick swipe and run was all that happened; they were all lucky that she was at the wrong place, or they might not have discovered the murder for a day or more.

Nick's legs felt like rubber walking back to the patrol car. He kept swinging his gaze left to right, right to left, far ground, near ground, the first verse to "Thriller" stuck in his head. More than once he stopped to search behind him, glad for the reach of his flashlight. He realized his voice was shaking when he checked in again with Simon at dispatch. This stretch of road, so welcoming and bucolic in daylight, was filled with shadows and ominous movement at night.

Nick spent the next few hours directing traffic and answering questions. As the other officers arrived, his fear dissipated, driven away by strength in numbers. A couple of the older guys from Lumbertown grasped his shoulder to show their support.

It was half past two when the Sergeant dismissed him with a gruff.

"Go get some sleep Moyers, and be back here at seven a.m. sharp. No dawdling this time." As if Nick needed a reminder—he'd started feeling guilty as soon as he got over the shock of finding the body. If he hadn't turned his call into a leisurely drive, he might have arrived in time to help Vommer.

By morning, it was all over the news. TV crews crowded the barricade that had been set up around the property. Adding media to the already stacked attraction of murder of a famed writer to the proximity to Halloween created an instant "made-for-TV-who-done-it" atmosphere. Already there was a steady stream of Lookie-Lou's driving by for a thrill.

Nick was asked to work with fellow officer Susan Kalowski and Detective Kyle Young from Lumbertown to review the details of the previous night and to start going through the evidence. After walking them through everything from the moment of his arrival to check on Stephanie, he honed in on the relevant details: broken lights along the driveway, house blazing with lights, broken vase and flowers near the front door, blood trail past a room filled with boxes and another with double doors firmly closed. Finally, in the study where he found the body, a fire still burning, fueled by what he assumed were manuscript pages. No obvious weapon, but he didn't examine the body closely enough to determine what might have caused the damage.

They started with the closed room and found it to be a small office, furnished sparsely with an ornate desk, chair, and credenza. The dust accumulating on the desk left a faint impression of a Laptop. The desk drawers held folding clips, pencils, highlighters, and Kleenex. The credenza held white copy paper of better quality than what Nick used at home. There was an antique oval rug on the floor. The small closet held a small red umbrella, a woman's coat, a hat, and gloves. There was a router in the closet, lights blinking to indicate that it was still functioning. A discreet door led to a small bathroom, what would have been called a "powder room" in this mansion. The basics—toilet paper, soap, a dry hand towel—indicated the room was sometimes still used for its intended purpose—or at least ready. All in all, the office didn't warrant further attention, so they moved on to the unmarked boxes across the wide hallway.

Young took charge and divided the piles of boxes roughly into thirds, and they got to work, silently going through rough drafts of books, the occasional screenplay, and copies of magazines with paperclips indicating a short story of Vommer's within. It was Kalowski who first noticed that there were some random drafts with notes in different handwriting—quite distinct from Vommer's almost illegible writing. After finding three of these drafts, she mentioned it to Nick and Young.

"Good catch," Young grunted. "Pull out any boxes that contain an anomaly and let's move those boxes over to this corner." To make sure they hadn't missed anything,

Young and Nick revisited the boxes they had already gone through.

Though unmarked, the boxes each contained about a year's worth of work. They started putting a note with the year on each box. Soon, it was apparent that Wommer had started using an assistant roughly fifteen years ago. Until that point, any handwritten notes or revisions were in Wommer's own hand. They started to notice that more and more of the handwritten notes were made by someone else, but there was never a name. This time, it was Nick who noticed a more subtle anomaly. For the past six or seven years, in every box, one draft had a different type font. Nick identified Wommer's font to be Times New Roman, the same one he personally preferred, but the random drafts were typed in Garamond. Vommer apparently used generic short titles for his works in progress: "Dwellers," "Boat," "Ancestors." The three manuscripts they found in Garamond all had one word titles beginning with the letter E: "Experiment," "Elements," and "Elevate."

They were on a short break when Nick, stretching his lower back, suddenly straightened and asked Young to look at the pages not consumed by the fire. Young immediately got where he was going and retrieved about a dozen bagged pages. They each took one and peered through the plastic bag to study the pages. Nick moved closer to the window. There was no name on these to differentiate them from the others, but on the left side of the bottom of each page were the initials "ce" in lower case, so faint that unless you were looking, you would never see them, especially since the eye is naturally drawn to the right. Kalowski checked the Garamond draft she had been looking at, and found that it, too, had the initials "ce" on the left side of each page. Young exhaled and, with a nod of approval to both Nick and Kalowski, said he'd better call his Captain Nick already had his hand on his phone and dialed before Young could. It rang twice before the Captain answered.

"Captain, I'll be honest, we don't have much to go on. Just some small stuff." Nick explained that they'd spent hours going through manuscript pages. By now it was mid-afternoon.

"Yeah, we found pages that don't match the authors type style and embossing in the left-hand corner of some of 'em, the letters ce. But, like I said, small stuff."

The captain agreed. "Yeah, let's get the coroner's report and interview Miss Wilson. Thoroughly. And find out who the assistant is."

Nick hung up the phone. "We'll finish these tomorrow I guess," he said nodding toward the remaining boxes. They all agreed.

"I'll see if we can't dig up some info on the assistant and the last time they met." Kowalski said, "See you later."

Once Young and Kowalski had left, Nick took a minute to observe the room. Nothing but boxes of pages. His mind wondered what it was like to be someone like Vommer, who was talented. Had money and fame, although he retreated from it. Moving to Colts Creek was a good way to keep him out of the spotlight. Even Rabbit Trapp road didn't get much traffic, which made wonder how many people really knew he was in this town.

And how many knew his exact address? So maybe it was someone he knew who was here that night. No forced entry. Nothing stolen- Nick stopped. Yes. There had been a laptop imprint on the desk in the other room, but no laptop was recovered. Where was that laptop and what was on it that was so important? Nick let his mind calculate an idea of who the real Vommer might be. What did he eat for breakfast? Did he have friends? Doubt it.

What was doing the day before? Or even earlier the day he was murdered? He paced the room. The lyrics to Thriller came echoing through his mind again. *You close your eyes and hope that this is just imagination/ Girl*....and just when the last word repeated itself in his mind he paused. *Girl.* There had been a woman's hat and gloves in the closet- the same room where the laptop had been. But, Vommer wasn't married. Someone was in too much of a hurry to grab their coat, hat, and gloves that night.

The next day, Nick let Young and Kowalski finish examining the remaining boxes of manuscripts while he took some time interviewing Stephanie Wilson, which proved to be fruitless. She had no recollection of what kind of car or color the car was. The only proof she had was her car's own scratched paint along her front bumper.

"I don't know how the heck I'm going to get to work while my car is in the shop. Gosh. I mean this is so hard to deal with. I'm having to borrow my Aunt's car which means I have to drop by her house every afternoon and socialize and feed her cats for her, you know? I don't want her to think I'm not grateful." She took plenty of time to vent her complaints and when Nick heard enough he thanked her and gladly left.

Next, he checked with the coroner's office but they too had no news yet. It would be another twenty-four hours before a final report was issued.

"C'mon Jules, gimme something," Nick said.

She huffed. "It looks like stab wounds, but I'm not officially saying that to you Nick. I'll call you when the report is ready." He thanked her and hung up the phone.

Nick had spent most of the night before sleepless, his mind full of images: the blood, the boxes of paper, the missing laptop, the letters *ce*. All of it started overlapping, and when he got a call from Kowalski, he hoped there had been a breakthrough.

"Vommer's last assistant died 6 years ago. And there's no contact info for anyone else after that. What doesn't make sense is that the manuscript writing that isn't Vommer's is definitely more recent." Now things seemed even more complicated.

Nick repeated her words. "There's no contact info for anyone else?"
"Nope, we found no personal phonebook. So, there's still no lead. But, you should know that he was scheduled to appear tonight, downtown in the square for a reading of his latest work- it's a Halloween picture book for kids. You know he loved kids," she said.

Nick ignored the last part of what she said. "Who exactly was the last person he had contact with?" he asked, agitated.

"You know, there's been no one to step forward since his murder. No family, just an editor who lives in New York. But I'll let you know if we find anything else."

"Alright. I'm heading over to the library," he said. Nick decided he'd take a stroll through downtown and let it all sink in on the way to the library. He strolled the sidewalks and took his time looking in shop windows.

There were topiaries outside boutique doors, pumpkins and autumn leaves strategically placed in front of the shop entranceways and windows. He waved to a few people and nodded to others.

The media was making their presence known. News teams huddled with cameras on every corner and several people stopped to talk, looking for their five minutes of fame. He did his best to avoid the crowds. When he finally rounded the corner of the library, he could see two news reporters and the library director, Tucheinne Endacott, talking with them. As he approached the reporters rushed over to him,

"Sir, can you comment on the murder of-"

"No. I believe Detective Young and the Colts Creek authorities have already stated that we have no comment at this time." He pushed past them both and Tuchienne gestured for him to follow her back inside.

"Officer, how are you?" she said as they walked through the library doors. "Let's step into my office," she said as if she had been expecting him.

"First, we are devastated about the news of Ralph. We considered him family and we all worked so closely together...." she stopped, unable to continue, overwhelmed by emotion. Nick cleared his throat, uncomfortable with her crying. He stumbled for words and pushed right to his questions, "Uh. Yeah. I understand."

"He was my friend. He and I worked so well together- he brought so much positive attention to the library. We've known each other for years. I helped him find a house here, even. And when he needed a personal recommendation.... for anything..." she stopped again, sniffing hard.

"Was there anything unusual with him lately, anything big or small?" Nick asked.

"He was getting older, you know. He started forgetting things and I think it started playing on his mind that he might not be mentally sound, not have all of his faculties about him, to write anymore award-winning books. He seemed agitated. Even short-tempered. But I just guess that was him under stress. He had a deadline too. Today. Halloween. I recommended that my daughter help him out a few times a week. But, that turned into almost every day. That's when I knew he was getting worse." She grabbed a tissue from her desk drawer and blew her nose.

"If you don't mind me asking, when was the last time you saw him? And your daughter, when was the last time she saw him?" he asked.

"Last Monday, here in the library. We were getting ready for the read-aloud that was scheduled for tonight. Then we talked about the events coming up next month and preparing a special event for Christmas. And I guess Sissy saw him...sometime last week. Her last year of college has been busy, so she was only visiting about once a week before the summer.

She manages the Little House of Books on Central, downtown." By now she was calm and Nick pressed on. She was very cooperative and answered all of his questions, even whether or not she had an alibi. Of course, she did.

"We were home that night. My husband and I spent the evening having dinner with our neighbors." When he had no other questions to ask, he politely thanked her and let himself out. So, Ralph Vommer did have friends, or a friend at least. And what seemed apparent to Nick was that the someone who rushed out of Vommer's house forgetting their coat and gloves, had the laptop, to stop Ralph from submitting a manuscript.

Tuchienne had mentioned that there was supposed to be a parade from the Little House of Books on the square to the downtown roundabout. There Vommer would've read his first book for kids. He walked back through the town center stopping at the Little House of Books. Perfect. He needed to question Sissy about the last time she was with Vommer.

He stepped through the small glass door and was in immediate view of a display of Vommer's Halloween book, *Spooky Boo.* He walked over to the table and picked up one of the books. Nick flipped through the pages--the story rhymed. He closed the book and put it back on the table. He watched as the kids lined up at the door, ready to march in the parade. A young woman came over and asked if he needed help. He told her he was wondering where he could find Sissy Endacott.

The woman stepped into a back room for a few minutes while Nick circled the shop. He ended up at the front desk which looked as though a paper bomb had exploded on top and underneath it. There were staples and paper notes stacked sloppily in the corner of the desk, and multiple coffee ring stains on top. A stack of paper clipped receipts had toppled over. A laptop was open while the cashier's computer was asleep. Nick noticed the typical desk supplies; post its, scissors, a letter opener, paper clips.

The phone rang but no one was there to answer. The store was empty by now with the all of the parents and their kids lined up outside anxiously waiting for the parade to start. Nick circled the store once again and this time when he came back around to the front desk he noticed a piece of paper underneath the laptop. There was the same writing he had seen at Vommer's. With no one watching he rounded the desk and pulled out the piece of paper. In the bottom, left hand corner were the letters *ce*. This was it. This is what he had been waiting for. A break. A big one.

Just when he grabbed his phone, a voice came from behind him. "He stole from me you know." A shaky angry voice said. It was a young woman, with her arms crossed. "He actually thought he could take my work. I worked so hard on every manuscript and he just…."

253

"Are you Sissy?" he was confused. She was in tears now pacing furiously around the store, ignoring his question.

"He just told me one day that he didn't need me anymore. And I demanded all of my work back. And when he wouldn't give it to me…" she was in hysterics now pulling at her hair.

"I went crazy. My name is Claire Endacott. I went crazy."

Jasper

Mildred Bledsoe, Stephanie Grattan, & Dennis Greeno

Jasper woke suddenly, out of breath. The clear blue sky swirled into view and the dank smell hit his nose so hard he started to cough. "Still here", he said to himself as sirens went off in the distance.

Jasper mused at the irony for a moment. He had spent his entire life trying to get out of Algiers and now he was literally stuck. It had been three days since the levees broke and the thing that was supposed to never happen, happened. New Orleans was under water.

Four Days Earlier

Sitting in the summer sun, Jasper could feel the skin melting off him. The humidity had been at strangling the city and everyone's temper was short. Through the screen door, Jasper could hear his Gramma yelling at the television, "No one gonna get me to leave my house, let me tell you. All this over a little rain, they out their minds. This mayor wanna act like he cares about us out here."

"She an angry woman", Jasper said to himself, half laughing. "You an angry woman Gramma!" She shouted back from the living room: "That may be so but I be angry in my own damn house!"

He couldn't think of laughing now, so he didn't. All he wanted to think about was getting off this roof. He started on his new morning routine, first yelling to the neighbors stuck in their attics. Once he had confirmed each of their voices, he adjusted his "HELP" sign.

There were plenty of helicopters coming through but few stopped. They would occasionally throw down bottles of water, some food; military rations so nasty Jasper

256

waited until the hunger cramps had him hunched over to eat them. He picked the mold off a piece of stale bread and ate it as fast as he could. He sat down, and he waited.

The looting started sooner than anyone could have guessed. Coming through on air mattresses and kiddie pools, bandanas covering their faces, they showed up everywhere and they took whatever they could find. Jasper silently thanked the old congressman on TV who had warned everyone to keep an axe close by. They all laughed then, calling him a crazy old redneck.

When the water started to bubble up through the gutters, Jasper grabbed the axe. As he broke the roof open, Jasper thought, "wasn't crazy – just a redneck." The axe kept the looters away, as did the old BB gun stuffed under some boxes in the attic. He had no ammo but the look of it was enough.

257

Day Four

Jasper grew bored staring out of the attic at the neighbors on roofs and the detritus floating in the mucky water. He started opening up a few of the boxes stacked in a dark corner of the attic – and spotted a trunk hidden by the shadows. Curious about the trunk, he pulled it under his improvised skylight and opened it. He tossed aside yellowed newspapers covering up a cardboard poster reading "Peg-Leg Portia's House of Delights". Jasper winced a bit as he spotted below the poster what looked like one of Gramma's old artificial legs mounted on a wooden base and covered with a black fishnet stocking.

"Jasper! Git over here and help me open this bottle of water!"

"Be right there, Gramma! I have something to show you!", Jasper shouted across the attic as he gathered up the poster and the "leg".

258

Portia Ambrose had raised Jasper as her own child after her daughter, K'Treena, died from a drug overdose shortly after giving birth. "Gramma" was a stern but nurturing presence in Jasper's life, but never spoke much about the years spent raising his mother. As far as Jasper can remember, Gramma always wore black stretchy trousers that covered up her artificial leg. As a boy, Jasper remembers watching Gramma take off the leg as part of her bedtime ritual.

"Gramma, look what I found in the attic!"

Gramma swallowed half of the water bottle, and burped after spotting the poster that Jasper waived in front of her. Her eyes followed the object emerging from behind Jasper's back while he hunched down to peck her on the cheek.

"Gramma, looks like "Portia" had fun with this sexy leg!" - doing his best imitation of Redd Foxx while setting the leg on top of the television like it was a valued trophy and tossing the poster on wooden floor beams.

"Jasper, what in the Sam Hill were you doin' messin' in my stuff? Put my stuff back where it belongs or I will clobber sense into you with my hammer!"

Jasper really didn't want to talk about the stuff, and climbed across the attic beams, carefully holding the leg and poster as if they were sacred objects.

The whirring of several helicopters caused Jasper to immediately poke his head out the make-shift skylight to see what was up. He reached for the HELP sign, but instead grabbed the stockinged leg and waived it to and fro. He spotted the logo of "News 13 NOLA" under the white belly of a copter hovering nearby. His heart pounded as he spotted the cameras on the copter aimed directly at him. A few second later, a second copter with a logo unfamiliar to Jasper scooted over and two men wearing Ray

Bans gave him the thumbs up signal. Jasper shot up his middle finger and yelled out "M……. Fkrs!"

Gramma overheard him cursing and yelled out to Jasper saying, "Boy didn't I tell you to put my stuff back?" In fact, "Peg-Leg Portia's House of Delights" was a storefront for "New Orleans Voodoo." While Jasper was waving the wooden leg in the air, there was a sudden appearance of white smoke and silver dust pouring out of the opening.

At first Jasper thought it was residual smoke from the helicopters until he saw the silver dust on his hands and arms. Jasper yelled out "Gramma, something strange is happening up here!" Suddenly he noticed a strange figure on the roof. This figure was wrapped from head to toe with what looked like a dirty white sheet. It was the figure of a woman with her mouth and eyes opened, and wearing a mask. He was very afraid and speechless.

Jasper mustered up the courage and called out to his gramma, "It's a Mummy on the roof!" "It's a Mummy on the roof!" Jasper threw the wooden leg down on the attic floor, and reached his hand out to close the hatch on the skylight. He stretched his arm and body as far as humanly possible however he was not strong enough to close the hatch. Jasper was frightened so much that he jumped off of the ladder and ran as fast as he could to get out of the attic. His heart was pounding like the constant beating of a drum. His sweat rolled off of him as if he had just stepped out of the shower. He scurried through the attic, screaming for Gramma to follow him. Jasper ran faster than he had done before, while crying out, "Gramma, help! Help! There is a mummy on the roof."

Gathering herself and timidly crossing the attic beams she yelled, "Boy what're you talkin' bout?!" Jasper grabbed hold of Gramma's arm and pulled her through the attic opening, landing on the second floor of their home - the floor the water had barely missed. Out of breath, Jasper gasped,

"Gramma, there was a mummy or somethin' up on that roof. I was messin' with that leg and saw smoke and then some lady, some mummy lookin' lady!" In the thirty-two years he had known her, Gramma was now the quietest she had ever been. Her eyes grew wide, like two milk saucers, and she stared at Jasper, slack jawed. "Gramma, you freakin' me out. Say somethin'." Then, she quietly whispered, "she's here."

Gramma started back towards the attic, with a new steely resolve. She spoke quickly, "Back when, we were running Portia's - the VooDoo Shop - your mother went and got herself into some trouble. Now I loved your Momma but she wasn't right, not since she was a little baby. She got herself in with a real bad men down the lower ninth." As she spoke, Gramma rummaged through box after box, flipping through books, and throwing them aside. "What're you lookin' for?!" "Boy! A little dark green book, now hush an' listen."

"So, your Momma got in with these men,

sellin' drugs and what not and I was desperate to get her away from em'. That's when ol' Loretta, you remember her, used to watch you when you were small. Loretta said she hada hex - get those boys away from your Momma real good. Jasper, I was so desperate-" At the bottom of a dusty grey box Gramma found the book she has been looking for. "Page thirty two, page thirty two"

"GRAMMA!" Jasper yelled, panicked at her silence. "We cut a deal! I promised her to shop if she could get rid of them men and she did, she laid that hex down on em'. Look out that door and tell me what she doin' out there." Jasper peeked his head out of the skylight hatch and saw the mummy approaching the skylight but ever so slowly, and with a slight limp. "She comin' Gramma, but she comin' slow."
"Good. Those men was gone but I went back on my word, I wouldn't give Loretta the shop. She never forgave me, ruined our friendship. Well, she got sick a few years after that. I went to make amends bein' a

good Christian an' all but she wouldn't hear it. She swore me a cursed life and said in my most desperate time of need she'd be back to haunt me, died a few days later. After that your Momma fell back in with drugs, you were born, and she passed. Shop went under, we had to sell. We were strugglin' all our life together, you had to grow up without and I never forgot it was my fault."

Jasper had heard enough, "What ya gonna do Gramma, she comin' for us?!" Gramma began to recite from the book, an old Creole incantation, "Rete! Atansyon! Ale vou zan! Ki te'm anrepo'm! Rete! Rete! Atansyon! Ale vou zan! Ki te'm anrepo'm! Rete! Rete! Atansyon! Ale vou zan! Ki te'm anrepo'm! Rete!" The mummy started to back away and grew more and more transpaprent. "Gramma! I think it's workin'!!"

"RETE! RETE! ATANSYON! ALE YOU ZAN! KI TE'M ANREPO'M! RETE! RETE! ATANSYON! ALE YOU ZAN! KI TE'M ANREPO'M! RETE! RETE! ATANSYON! ALE YOU ZAN! KI TE'M ANREPO'M!" The more Gramma said the incantation, the quicker the mummy began to dissolve. Soon, she disappeared in a cloud of white smoke as strangely as she had first appeared. Gramma collapsed, exhausted and with all the color drained from her face she laid across the roof shingles. Jasper leaned down to her,"I'm so sorry baby" she murmured raspy and quiet. "I brought this on us, I brought all this misfortune on us and on you and your life. I'm sorry baby, I'm so sorry."

"Gramma, you saved my life. Without you, where would I be at? With a Momma on drugs or thrown in the system? Gramma, you saved me. An' I'm gonna save you. We gonna get out of here, Gramma. We gonna be alright."

Made in the USA
Columbia, SC
20 October 2017